PROJECTION EDGE

PROJECTION EDGE

VOLUME 2

THOMAS K. DYE

The characters of Eva and Eamonn would have not been possible without the assistance of Emily Koehler-Platten and Rory O'Bannion, respectively.

Japanese translations courtesy Ryan Gates.

Many thanks to Allan Dye, Teiran and Fuzzwolf of Furplanet, Chris Crosby and Teri Crosby of Keenspot, and the love of my life Tim Tylor. Also many thanks to the fans who keep reading and keep believing in the worlds I create!

Dedicated to the Patreon patrons who help keep the comic alive!

Thanks to:

Dana Simpson, David K. Pratt, Joel A. S. Butler, Minzoku, Gildedtongue,
Mabel Greysmoke, Tyrnn, Jon Helfrich, Tapewolf, T'Chall,
Tazel "Sixpaws" Tanner, Alan Foreman, Wilford B. Wolf, Eric Schissel, Dipper,
Ryan Dewalt, Austin Dern, Punktiger, The City of Elseways, Bitter Karella,
Tenax Raccoon, Mark Smith, Moult, Kaoru Greendrake, Jarad,
and all the remaining patrons who help fuel the Projection Edge
momentum!

PRIMARY CAST

EVA - A Canadian terrier mix, formerly owned by Miranda Hayes, now in care of her sister Shelley Hayes. She is an explorer of the plane known as the Projection Edge.

EAMONN - An Irish setter, a former service animal bought by Miranda Hayes and also now in care of her sister. He is considered particularly adept with the Projection Edge, although there is some mystery behind him.

BIJOU - A mixed-breed test animal for Neurosmith, a psychological think tank and research laboratory.

QUENBY - A Field Spaniel mix, the mascot for Friendstream, a premier social media platform. The company is vaguely aware of her psychic abilities.

MARCEL GODCHAUX - A veterinary student hired by Friendstream to be Quenby's primary handler.

MIRANDA HAYES - A premier yoga expert curious about Eva's Projection Edge experiences.

GARRETT HILLMAN - Miranda's right-hand man who betrays her and tries to sell Eva and Eamonn.

GIDEON BEST - The wunderkind behind Neurosmith, who planned to sell majority control to CCC, a conservative megacorporation. He dies under mysterious circumstances.

THE REVEREND - A Doberman mix, and Gideon's "spiritual advisor." He eventually leads a group of dogs known as the "Chosen Souls."

KINGMAKER - A Persian cat assigned by Gideon Best to replicate Quenby's psychic nature in other dogs. His project is usurped by the Reverend as the canine test subjects become the "Chosen Souls."

BUDDY - A border collie, another test animal at Neurosmith and a friend of Bijou's.

ARTHUR - A tabby kitten, also another Neurosmith test animal and friend of Bijou's.

NELLIE DUNCAN - A Neurosmith scientist trying to exploit Bijou's use of the Projection Edge. She was also grifting money from the head of CCC Incorporated, before being fired from Neurosmith and spiraling into a mental breakdown.

ADAM JAMESON - Another Neurosmith scientist.

HIKARU - A Japanese bulldog who has had a past connection to the Projection Edge.

SHELLEY HAYES - Miranda Hayes' sister who, at the end of the last volume, takes in Eva, Eamonn, Bijou, and later, Quenby.

Enjoy the story!
Thomas K. Dye
May 2023

chow
'n
chava
chow
'n
chava

CHAPTER 9 "HAPPY NEW YEAR"
WELP. OVER THE COLUMBIA RIVER NOW. WELCOME TO WASHINGTON. ONE HOUR TO YELM.
YOU OKAY?

...IT JUST HIT ME. I'M MOVING TO A NEW STATE BECAUSE I'VE JUST BEEN SOLD FROM A SOCIAL MEDIA GIANT TO A FAMOUS WRITER. *YOU* JUST UPROOTED YOUR ENTIRE LIFE TO WORK AT A SMALL TOWN VET. ALL BECAUSE OF SOMETHING I USED TO THINK WAS SO *ORDINARY.* UNTIL NOW I'VE *TRIED* TO BE CALM AND COLLECTED. NOW, I'M *SCARED.*

...I WOULDN'T SAY THAT I HAD MUCH OF A LIFE TO UPROOT.
STILL...

STILL, YOU'LL FEEL BETTER WHEN YOU REJOIN YOUR FRIENDS, AND WE CAN GET THIS SORTED OUT *TOGETHER.*

Yelm
ELEV 354 ft
POP 16,154

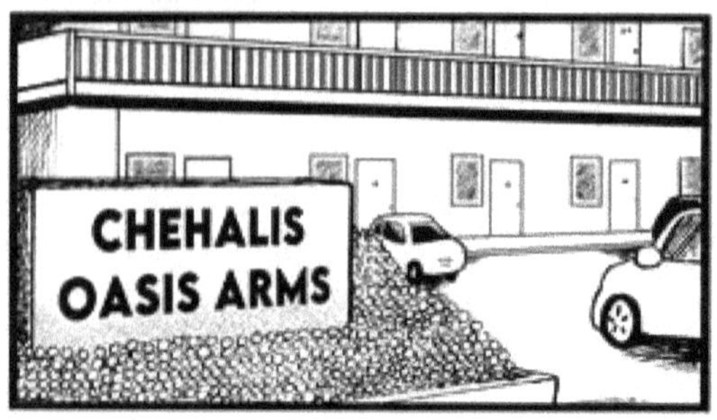

CHEHALIS
OASIS ARMS

I MEAN, I WAS USED TO QUESTIONING. THAT BIZARRE CAT DID IT TO ME EVERY WEEK.

... BUT THIS WAS DIFFERENT.
I DON'T CARE HOW YOU BLEW OFF KINGMAKER.
YOU'RE NOT GOING TO IGNORE ME.

HE WOULDN'T BELIEVE ME. HE THOUGHT I HAD SOME SECRET CODE MEMORIZED THAT I WAS KEEPING FROM HIM AND THAT CAT. I WAS SO GLAD TO GET OUT OF THERE.
GOOD!

DID YOU HAVE A NICE TRIP?
... OH, YES, MA'AM.

QUENBY, THIS IS SHELLEY HAYES.
PLEASED TO MEET YOU, MA'AM.
...LIKEWISE.

AHEM

I'LL BE BLUNT.

I DON'T CARE MUCH FOR MY SISTER'S PHILOSOPHY, BUT I DO CARE ABOUT HER. SHE MADE YOUR DESPERATE SITUATION QUITE CLEAR AND YOUR PRESENCE HERE WILL REMAIN A SECRET.
BUT THIS IS ALL PAID FOR BY SIX NOVELS A YEAR, AND THEY CAN'T GET WRITTEN BY SOMEONE WHO'S DISTRACTED BY A LOT OF DOG SHENANIGANS.
SO BE AWARE I HAVE GROUND RULES. DO NOT BOTHER ME IN THE OFFICE UNLESS THE HOUSE IS ON FIRE. GO TO GISELE FOR ALL YOUR NEEDS. SHE'S AGREED TO HELP.
IN SHORT, BEHAVE YOURSELF, KEEP QUIET, AND EVERYTHING WILL BE FINE.

SLAM!

SHE... GAVE US THAT SPEECH TOO. SHE'S FINE.
SHE EVEN BUILT ME A TETHERBALL COURT!
I'M STILL MORE COMFORTABLE HERE THAN I'VE BEEN AT FRIENDSTREAM FOR THE LAST SIX WEEKS.

REMEMBER, WHEN ARPHAXAD BEGAT SALAH, THAT MEANS HE DIDN'T BEGET CANAAN, ALTHOUGH YOU COULD SAY IN A WAY HE BEGAT EZEKIAS AND MANASSES. BUT LET'S RETURN TO SERUG AND NAHOR. IN THE YEARS THAT TERAH LIVED AS NAHOR'S SON, DID HE REGRET NOT BEGETTING HARAN BEFORE ABRAM? THIS THEOLOGICAL PUZZLE TRULY GIVES ONE PAUSE. FOR HE MAY HAVE THOUGHT BACK TO HOW EBER BEGAT PELEG KNOWING FULL WELL THAT JOKTAN BEGAT ALMODAD. THINK ABOUT THAT.
GOD BLESS YOU ALL AND GOOD NIGHT.

THAT'S AMAZING, ISN'T IT?
NO!

WHAT DOES ALL THAT HAVE TO DO WITH ANYTHING?!

WHAT DO YOU MEAN?
EIGHT WEEKS OF BIBLE STUDY, AND I STILL DON'T SEE HOW IT RELATES TO WHAT'S HAPPENING TO US EVERY NIGHT!

WHAT THE—? WE'RE GETTING CLOSER TO GOD!
WE'RE GETTING CLOSER TO CRAZY!

"... DON'T LOOK AT ME LIKE THAT."

I'M NOT NUTS. THIS "GOD" STUFF IS MEANINGLESS.
IT DOESN'T EXPLAIN WHAT'S HAPPENING AT ALL.

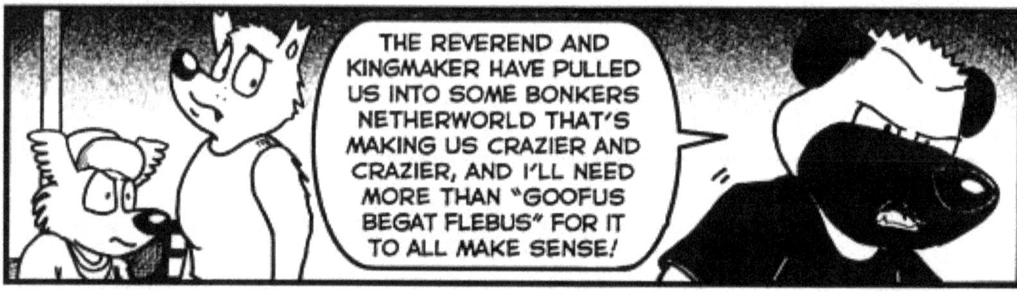

THE REVEREND AND KINGMAKER HAVE PULLED US INTO SOME BONKERS NETHERWORLD THAT'S MAKING US CRAZIER AND CRAZIER, AND I'LL NEED MORE THAN "GOOFUS BEGAT FLEBUS" FOR IT TO ALL MAKE SENSE!

LATER THAT NIGHT
... THEY DID IT. THEY SOLD QUENBY. SHE'S GONE.
I'M NOT SURPRISED.
YOUR PRESENCE IN THAT OFFICE WASN'T SUBTLE.

IT DOESN'T MATTER. SHE WAS AN INFORMATIONAL VOID ANYWAY.
LIKE I TOLD YOU.

THE CHOSEN SOULS ARE MAKING PROGRESS. WE'LL JUST HAVE TO BE PATIENT.

COME ON, LITTLE FELLA. GET UP.

WHAT'S THE MATTER, BUDDY?
WE'RE LEAVING NEUROSMITH. FOR GOOD.

WHAT? BUT WHY?
WE'RE JUST NOT WANTED ANYMORE, LITTLE GUY.

NOT WANTED?
I'LL EXPLAIN LATER, I PROMISE. BUT WE HAVE TO LEAVE.
BEEP BEEP
BEEP

BEEP BEEP BEEEEEEEEEEEP
CHUNK

BUT...

WHAT ABOUT ADAM?

I'M SORRY, ADAM. NELLIE'S PROJECT HAS SOURED MANAGEMENT ON ANY FURTHER ANIMAL-BASED RESEARCH. IF YOU WANT TO HAVE A HAND IN YOUR ANIMALS' ULTIMATE FATE, YOU'D BETTER SPEAK UP NOW.

THAT'S ABOUT IT. WE'VE FAXED ALL YOUR PAPERS TO CORPORATE SO ONCE THEY'RE PROCESSED YOU CAN BEGIN TOMORROW MORNING!
THANK YOU!
DOG
CAT
Chehalis
PET CARE

DO YOU HAVE ANY MORE QUESTIONS FOR ME?
MMM... ONE.

BACK IN SCHOOL I'D TAKEN A COURSE ON CANINE NEUROLOGICAL DISORDERS. IT MADE ME THINK...IF A DOG OR CAT NEEDED AN MRI, WHERE WOULD WE GO?

WELL, USUALLY WE OUTSOURCE THAT TO OLYMPIA, THOUGH THAT'S RARE. MOST OFTEN, THEIR OWNERS PREFER...
... YOU KNOW.
I UNDERSTAND.

I MEAN, WE RECOMMEND WHATEVER TREATMENT'S NECESSARY, OF COURSE, BUT IT'S RARE THAT THEY CONSIDER IT ONCE WE MENTION THE COST.
UNDERSTOOD.

...SHE'LL LIVE. JUST NEXT TIME DON'T CHEW SO HARD.
OH YES...
THE "COST..."

HELLO! PLEASE ANSWER ME! PLEASE!

GIVE THIS UP.

IT'S BEEN THREE WEEKS. I HAVEN'T ASKED FOR A THING.
PLEASE LET ME BACK INTO THAT WORLD AGAIN.
SON...
LET ME EXPLAIN THIS TO YOU FOR THE LAST TIME...

YOU MUST STOP BEING DEPENDENT ON ME. YOUR EXPERIENCE HERE IS NOT MEANT TO BE AN INTERACTIVE NARCOTIC.
YOU NEED TO LIVE YOUR OWN LIFE.

BUT MY LIFE IS HELL! I'M STAYING WITH MY CRACKHEAD SISTER WHO'S ALREADY ON MY CASE ABOUT MY SLEEPING DURING THE DAYTIME!
YOU HAVE TO HELP ME!
I CAN'T.
THIS HAS TO STOP.
I'M ON A SEARCH OF MY OWN. YOUR "DREAM ENVIRONMENT" IS ON THE EDGE OF FALLING INTO CHAOS AND I NEED TO FIND OUT WHY. GOODBYE, GARRETT.

BUT...
LIVE YOUR OWN LIFE.

HE CAN'T DO THIS TO ME.
I CAN'T KEEP GOING TO SLEEP AND ENDING UP HERE...

...ALONE.

"ON A SEARCH?"

LET ME GO WITH YOU!!
I CAN HELP!!!

LET ME GO WITH—
SLAM

ALL RIGHT, GET YOUR LAZY ASS OFF THE COUCH. MY BOOK CLUB'S COMING OVER AND I HAVEN'T EVEN READ "A CONFEDERACY OF DUNCES" YET.

I SWEAR, NORAH, I DIDN'T GIVE BUDDY AND ARTHUR THE CODES.
THEN HOW DID THEY GET OUT? I.T.'S NOT IN THE HABIT OF GIVING OUT DOOR CODES TO ANIMALS.
NORAH JANE STOKES
CAMPUS DIRECTOR

SIGH HOW INVOLVED WERE THAT CAT AND DOG WITH NELLIE'S WORK?
BIJOU MIGHT HAVE TALKED WITH THEM, BUT THAT'S ALL.

THEY WERE WITH YOU WHEN YOU FOUND BIJOU IN HER OFFICE, WEREN'T THEY?
... YES, THAT'S TRUE.

I DON'T THINK WE SHOULD LET THIS GO BUT THERE'S HONESTLY NOT A LOT WE CAN DO. IF IT GETS OUT THAT WE'RE LOOKING FOR THEM, THEY COULD SPILL WHAT THEY KNOW ABOUT WHAT NELLIE'S BEEN DOING.
I KNOW THEM, AND I DON'T THINK THEY'D DO THAT.

MAYBE WE CAN DISCREETLY INFORM ANIMAL CONTROL. IN THE MEANTIME, LET'S ALERT OUR LEGAL DEPARTMENT AND HOLD ON FOR DEAR LIFE.
HOW DID THEY GET THE DOOR CODES?

...THEY'RE WAITING FOR ME.

... OKAY, ENOUGH.
I'VE PUT THIS OFF FOR TWO WEEKS. I CAN'T PUT IT OFF ANY LONGER. THE WHOLE REASON I'M HERE IS TO FIND OUT ABOUT THIS THING OF THEIRS.
... SO LET'S GO.

"THIS FEELS SO ODD AFTER LEAVING IT ALONE FOR TWO MONTHS."
"DOESN'T FEEL AS FAMILIAR AS IT USED TO, NO."

HEY, GUYS! YOU ALL READY?
WELL, LET'S NOT RUSH IT, WE DON'T WANT TO SCARE MARCEL OR ANYTHING...

OOPS... TOO LATE.

HOLY CRAP.
UH, SORRY. I THINK BIJOU WAS A BIT EXCITED...

...IS THIS WHAT YOU DID EVERY NIGHT?
UP UNTIL WE LEFT MINNESOTA, WHEN YOU TOLD US TO STOP.

SO SPEAK TO US, LAD. NOW THAT YOU'RE HERE, WHAT IS IT YOU'RE WORRIED ABOUT?
WAIT... WHAT'S HAPPENING...?

THIS IS, LIKE, WHAT MAKES YOU FEEL AT PEACE?
WHAT IS IT?

IT'S... MY VISION OF A PERFECT FUTURE WORLD.
... MINUS A DETAIL OR TWO, I GUESS.
YCH

THIS IS AMAZING.
I CAN'T SEE ANYTHING WRONG WITH IT.
YOU'VE ALL CREATED A MIRACLE.

WELL, WE DIDNT REALLY CREATE--
IT'S PERFECT. I FEEL SO... BLESSED.

YOU WON'T WHEN YOU'RE AWAKE, THOUGH. YOU'VE GOT TO PAY ATTENTION. WE NEED TO KNOW WHY YOU'RE SO CONCERNED ABOUT THIS.
HEY...

WHAT'S "CNS" STAND FOR?
CNS...
CNS

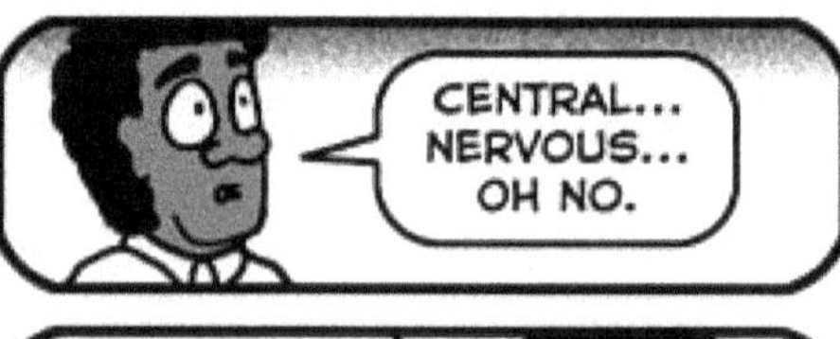

CENTRAL... NERVOUS... OH NO.

OH, Y'ALL... BRINGING THIS UP IS KILLING MY MELLOW...

I KNOW WHAT'S HAPPENING.

THERE'S A CRAZY AMOUNT OF UNUSUAL NEUROTRANSMITTER ACTIVITY GOING ON. SEROTONIN, DOPAMINE, EPINEPHRINE... AND THAT'S JUST THE ONES I FEEL NOW.

WHAT DOES THAT MEAN, EXACTLY?
NOT ALL OF THIS ACTIVITY IS BENEFICIAL.

"IT'S MULTIDIMENSIONAL DOMINOES HERE... THESE EUPHORIC REACTIONS ARE TOPPLING OVER OTHER NATURAL NEURAL MECHANISMS, CREATING HIDDEN AND POTENTIALLY DAMAGING EFFECTS."
WHAT? THAT CAN'T BE. DON'T TALK RUBBISH.
NO, NO... I NEED TO TELL YOU MORE, BUT MY BRAIN IS ANESTHETIZING ME FROM MY MAKING ANY MORE CONCLUSIONS...

HOW ARE YOU DOING THIS?!
WHAT!!

LET GO OF ME! I DON'T KNOW!
TELL ME!

I HAVE TO KNOW BEFORE —
...OH, SNAP.

HE'S MAD!!!

HE'S UTTERLY MAD!!

IS HE?

HE DOESN'T *KNOW.* HE JUST THINKS THAT NOTHING GOOD CAN HAPPEN WITHOUT A *PRICE.*
NEXT QUESTION.

WHY DID HE IMMEDIATELY ASK *YOU* HOW YOU WERE DOING THIS, INSTEAD OF ALL OF US?
CRACK

TIME'S UP. THE ANSWER IS IT'S *OBVIOUS* YOU'RE GAINING *MORE CONTROL* OVER WHATEVER'S IN YOU THAT'S EXPANDING THE RANGE OF THE PROJECTION EDGE. BUT HEY, THAT'S A-OK, ISN'T IT? AFTER ALL, *YOU* INTEND TO USE IT STRICTLY FOR *GOOD.*

SO, GENEROUSLY, YOU AGREED TO WAIT, BIDING YOUR TIME PLAYING TETHERBALL WITH BIJOU AND RESEARCHING DOMESTIC ANIMAL EVOLUTION WITH ME...

"...AS LONG AS YOU *LIKED* WHAT MARCEL HAD TO SAY."

I SUPPOSE IF MARCEL CAN'T BE CONVINCED TO SEE YOUR SIDE OF THIS, "EAMONN THE FIRE GOD" WILL INVOKE HIS WRATH AND TORMENT HIM IN HIS SLEEP. STRICTLY FOR GOOD. THE WAY YOU "ENCOURAGED" MY ENGULFMENT IN FLAMES. *STRICTLY FOR GOOD.*
I NEVER ASKED FOR THIS! I WAS HAPPY HELPING OTHERS BEFORE YOU GOT ME INVOLVED IN THIS *BLOODY GAME!!*

SHALL WE STOP ALTOGETHER THEN? ALL OF US. JUST STOP. FFFT!

OH NO. THERE'S NO *WAY* THAT *YOU* WOULD *EVER* STOP.

DON'T TEMPT ME.

ADAM? HI, THIS IS MARCEL GODCHAUX. REMEMBER ME, THE VET STUDENT WITH QUENBY? I'M SORRY TO WAKE YOU SO EARLY, BUT ... NO, BIJOU'S FINE. THIS IS ABOUT SOMETHING ELSE. IT'S VERY IMPORTANT.

I NEED TO KNOW WHAT MEDICALLY HAPPENED TO NELLIE DUNCAN *RIGHT AWAY.*

VISCO - CITY
chow 'n' c[how]
C'MON, LITTLE FELLA. YOU HAVEN'T EATEN SINCE YESTERDAY.
I'M TOO SCARED TO EAT, BUDDY. I'VE NEVER BEEN SO FAR FROM HOME BEFORE.

NEUROSMITH ISN'T OUR HOME ANYMORE, LI'L GUY. WE WERE TEST ANIMALS. AND WHEN WE WEREN'T NEEDED ANYMORE, WELL...

... THEY WERE GOING TO GET RID OF US.
ADAM WOULDN'T HAVE LET THAT HAPPEN.
chow 'n' chow

ADAM WORKS FOR THEM. AFTER THE NELLIE THING, HE'S NOT GOING TO JEOPARDIZE HIS CAREER.
I STILL DON'T BELIEVE THAT.
chow 'n' chow

C'MON, ARTHUR! CHIN UP!
MF!

IF EVA AND EAMONN CAN GO HALFWAY ACROSS THE COUNTRY BY THEMSELVES, SO CAN WE, RIGHT? C'MON, EAT YOUR SANDWICH.
BUT WE DON'T EVEN KNOW WHERE WE'RE GOING!

I DO.
JUST TRUST ME.

EXIT
CLOP
CLOP CLOP
CLOP CLOP
CLOP

CLOP CLOP
CLOP CLOP
CLOP CLOP
CLOP

... MAY I HELP YOU?

SO YOU'RE THE "KINGMAKER," ARE YOU?
JUST "KINGMAKER."

I DON'T DO PRETENTIOUS DEFINITE ARTICLES THE WAY THE REVEREND DOES.
YES... THE "REVEREND."

I SUPPOSE HE'S TOLD YOU OF HIS SPECIAL RELATIONSHIP TO FRIENDSTREAM.
I BELIEVE HE CONSIDERS HIMSELF A REPRESENTATIVE OF THE LATE MR. BEST'S INTERESTS.

WE'LL BE DIRECT.
HE'S BEEN A THORN IN FRIENDSTREAM'S SIDE EVER SINCE MR. BEST PASSED AWAY.
WITH QUENBY GONE, WE HAD ASSUMED WE WOULD BEGIN THE PROCESS OF FORCING HIM OUT OF FRIENDSTREAM'S CORPORATE DECISION-MAKING.

"...UNTIL WE FOUND OUT ABOUT YOUR REAL 'PROJECT.'"

THANK YOU FOR TALKING WITH ME, MS. DUNCAN.
I DON'T KNOW HOW I CAN HELP.
"THIS ALL RELATES TO THE RESEARCH NELLIE WAS DOING. I MIGHT BE ABLE TO FIND SOME WAY TO HELP HER. I JUST NEED TO KNOW WHAT CONDITION SHE'S IN."
SIGH WHY NOT TELL YOU.

"WE STARTED HOSPICE THIS MORNING."
HOSPICE?!

SHE HAS SOMETHING LIKE ADVANCED LEWY BODY DEMENTIA.
WHAT?!

"SOMETHING LIKE IT. HER DOCTOR HASN'T BEEN ABLE TO PIECE IT TOGETHER FROM HER MEDICAL HISTORY, BUT WHEN YOUR MRIs LOOK THAT BAD, THE QUESTION IS MOOT, ISN'T IT?"

"I'M... SO SORRY."
"WAS THAT WHAT YOU NEEDED?"

"YES... I'M SORRY. PLEASE CALL ME IF YOU NEED ANYTHING."
"I DOUBT THAT WILL BE NECESSARY ..."

"... BUT THANK YOU."

"...ANYWAY, I THOUGHT YOU SHOULD KNOW."
I APPRECIATE YOUR LOYALTY.

PFFT. I HATE THOSE PEOPLE.
AT THE SAME TIME, MAYBE YOU SHOULDN'T HAVE BEEN SO HIGH-PROFILE WHEN YOU WERE INTERROGATING QUENBY.
YOU MAY HAVE BEEN RIGHT.

"THE ANSWER IS SIMPLE. YOU FIND A WAY TO FUND THIS, WE DON'T NEED FRIENDSTREAM ANYMORE."

OH, FRIENDSTREAM DOESN'T HOLD ALL THE CARDS, EVEN IF THEY THINK THEY DO. STILL... IT'S TIME WE CHANGED OUR BUSINESS MODEL.
WHAT DO YOU MEAN?

IT IS TIME, CHOSEN SOULS, FOR YOU TO GO OUT INTO THE WORLD AND SPREAD THE WORD OF THE LORD'S MIRACLE!!
YES, REVEREND!
HALLELUJAH!
HALLELUJAH!

DO YOU *KNOW* WHAT ADVANCED LEWY BODY DEMENTIA IS?
IT'S...LIKE PARKINSON'S, ISN'T IT?

PHEW. THAT "PROJECTION EDGE" OF YOURS IS NOT HELPING YOU IN THE *RIGHT WAYS.* IT IS A SYNUCLEO-PATHIC DISEASE CAUSED BY MISFOLDED PROTEINS.

IT TAKES *YEARS* TO DEVELOP THE SYMPTOMS OF IT, AND FROM WHAT HER MOTHER TOLD ADAM, NOTHING IN HER PRIOR MEDICAL HISTORY INDICATED HER SUSCEPTIBILITY TO THE DISEASE.
"BUT ONE OF THE EARLIEST INDICATORS IS *REM SLEEP BEHAVIOR DISORDER,* WHICH CAN HAPPEN *YEARS* BEFORE THE ONSET OF DEMENTIA WITH LEWY BODIES."

NOW WHAT NELLIE HAS IS "SOMETHING SIMILAR" SO THIS ISN'T AN EXACT DIAGNOSIS. HOWEVER, MY THEORY, BASED ON MY EXPERIENCE WITH YOU, IS THAT SHE GOT AN ENORMOUS AND CONCENTRATED BURST OF F***ED UP PROTEIN ACTIVITY IN THE NIGHT, AND THAT HASTENED HER CURRENT CONDITION IN A WAY NO ONE HAS *EVER SEEN.*

"DO YOU... GET... ME?"

DO YOU MEAN... WE DID THAT TO NELLIE?!
AND MAYBE KAYLA...

AND SARAH, AND JORDAN, AND PHOEBE, AND DEREK, NOT TO MENTION ROBIN...
THAT'S A BLOODY LIE! WHEN WE VISITED THEM, I DIDN'T—

LISTEN. WE'VE BEEN PLAYING BY YOUR RULES REGARDING THE PROJECTION EDGE LONG ENOUGH. YOU KNOW MORE THAN YOU'RE LETTING ON. SO START TALKING...

...YOU DIDN'T WHAT, EAMONN?

"...OR I AM DONE."

ARE WE REALLY NEARLY THERE?
YEP, LI'L GUY. NOT MUCH FARTHER NOW.
Yelm   10 mi
Puyallup   45 mi
Kirkland   85 mi

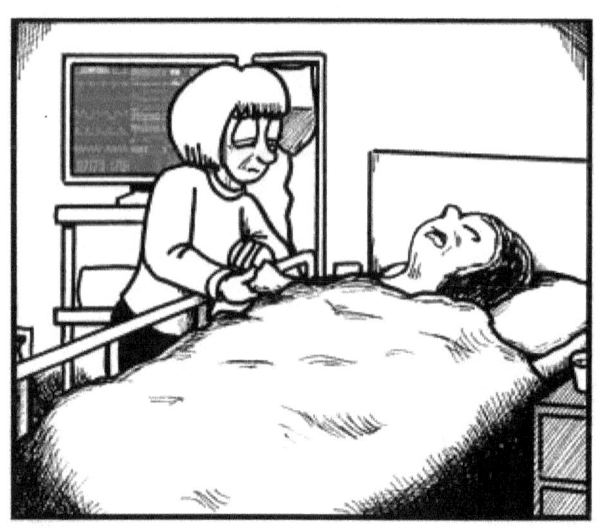

HELLO?
HELLO, IS THAT MRS. BEATRICE DUNCAN?
YES... WHO IS SPEAKING?
YOUR DAUGHTER GAVE ME YOUR NUMBER AS AN EMERGENCY CONTACT. I'VE HEARD ABOUT YOUR DAUGHTER'S CONDITION AND I WISHED TO EXPRESS MY DEEPEST SYMPATHIES.
WELL, THANK YOU... BUT WHO IS THIS?

MY NAME IS PRUDENCE LA SALLE...
I AM THE PRESIDENT OF CCC INTERNATIONAL.

CHAPTER 10
"TALE OF THE KILNS"
HA! I TOLD YOU THAT WAS THE BIG DIPPER, EAMONN!
AH, WHAT DO I KNOW, ALL THE STARS LOOK THE SAME TO ME.

AH, LADS, HOW ABOUT HEADING BACK TO EARTH, I'M A BIT TIRED.
THAT'D BE GRAND, BOGS!
TAKE US TO CALIFORNIA!

CALIFORNIA'S A BIG PLACE!
TAKE US SOMEWHERE WHERE WE CAN SEE WHALES!

LOOK AT THEM THERE!
THEY'VE ALL COME TO SEE US!

BOGS! LET'S GO RIDE ONE!
AH, COME NOW, THEY WOULDN'T BE LIKIN' THAT, WOULD THEY?
BESIDES, YOU'LL ALL BE WAKIN' NOW...

THANKS FOR BRINGING ME ALONG, EAMONN! I HAD A LOVELY TIME!
SEE YOU AGAIN SOON!

I REMEMBER THEM ALL... MY BROTHERS, NIALL AND SULLY...
OUR FRIENDS, CIARA, KENT, EOWYN, HUMPHREY... HE WAS FROM AMERICA...
NEVER SAW OUR FRIENDS IN REAL LIFE BUT I ALWAYS SAW THEM AT NIGHT.

I WISH I COULD CONJURE THE FEELING I HAD AS EASILY AS I CAN CONJURE THEIR NAMES...

THE ELDERLY WIDOW WHO OWNED ME AND MY BROTHERS DIED WHEN I WAS TOO WEE TO REMEMBER. AT THAT POINT HER SON, A MAN NAMED MILES DONNELLY, CAME BACK FROM AMERICA TO CLAIM HER HOUSE IN WICKLOW... AND CARE FOR US.

"I REMEMBER VERY LITTLE ABOUT HIM APART FROM HIS HOBBY OF WORKING WITH CLAY..."

THERE WERE RUMOURS IN THE NEIGHBOURHOOD THAT HE'D ALSO, SHALL WE SAY, STAYED IN AMERICA A BIT TOO LONG. HE'D FOREWENT HIS CATHOLIC UPBRINGING AND GONE HIS OWN PECULIAR WAY.

"...BUT THAT WAS NEITHER HERE NOR THERE TO US."
HEY!

YOU'RE IN QUITE THE HURRY.
OH, SORRY, MR. DONNELLY! I'M RIGHT HAPPY OUT! EAMONN, SULLY AND I HAD A WONDERFUL DREAM!

WHAT DO YOU MEAN?
WE DREAM TOGETHER! WE CAN DO AMAZING THINGS!

"... DREAM TOGETHER?"
YOU SHOULD COME JOIN US!

"SO NIALL WANTED DONNELLY TO JOIN US. I WAS YOUNG AND THOUGHT, 'WHAT'S THE HARM?'"

SO YOU KNEW YOU COULD INVOLVE HUMANS BACK THEN.
I DIDN'T HAVE A DAMNED CLUE ABOUT ANY OF YOUR "RULES." I JUST KNEW I COULD MAKE IT SO HE'D BE WITH US.

"...SO I DID."
WHAT DO YOU THINK, MR. DONNELLY?
IS IT NOT GRAND?
WHERE WOULD YOU LIKE TO GO? BOGS CAN TAKE US ANYPLACE!
WELCOME MR. DONNELLY
WELCOME MR. DONNE
WELCOM MR. DONNEL
wel mr. d

...THIS IS SHEOL.

THE LORD IS MY SHEPHERD; I SHALL NOT WANT. HE MAKETH ME LIE DOWN IN GREEN PASTURES... HE LEADETH ME BESIDE THE STILL WATERS...

EAMONN? WHAT'S HAPPENING?
WHAT'S GOING ON?!
"I KNEW."

"OR AT LEAST I KNEW WHY IT WAS HAPPENING. DONNELLY WAS UPSET. I COULDN'T UNDERSTAND IT, BUT I TRUSTED HIM. I LET IT HAPPEN."

"HE WAS OUR HUMAN. HE CARED FOR US AND FED US. HE'D BE ALL RIGHT, SURELY."

"ONCE WE WOKE UP, NIALL AND SULLY CAME TO ME IN FEAR. I TRIED TO CONVINCE THEM THAT EVERYTHING WAS FINE, HE WASN'T USED TO IT, BLAH BLAH BLAH..."

YOU SEE, I'D DECIDED I WOULD KEEP BRINGING HIM IN UNTIL WE GOT IT RIGHT.

PAF!

... AND WE WOULD GET IT RIGHT.

"I TRIED EVERYTHING! BOGS TOOK US TO FRANCE, ITALY, GALILEE, THE FLIPPING GARDEN OF EDEN... BUT DONNELLY'S MADNESS ONLY GREW WORSE AND WORSE."

"IN THE WAKING WORLD, DONNELLY KEPT AWAY FROM US OR SPOKE TO US HARSHLY... NEVER IN FRONT OF GUESTS, OF COURSE... BUT THE THREE OF US WERE SHAKEN BY HOW HE'D CHANGED."

"YET ALL THE TIME I WAS CERTAIN I COULD MEND THIS, AND MR. DONNELLY WOULD GET IT."

"ON THE SEVENTH NIGHT... SULLY AND NIALL WERE NO LONGER HAPPY... BOGS HAD BECOME SOMETHING ILL AND DISEASED... AND JUST AS I WAS TRYING TO CONVINCE DONNELLY TO RELAX, HE LUNGED FORWARD AND ATTACKED US."
"...I WAS DONE."

"I WANTED TO BURN IT ALL DOWN..."

"...AND START OVER."

"AND THEN..."

"DONNELLY SNAPPED."

HALLELUJAH!!

WHEN I WOKE UP, I NOTICED MY BROTHERS WERE NOT THERE. I HEARD A POUNDING.

"IT SEEMED TO TAKE AN ETERNITY FOR ME TO RUN OUT OF THE ROOM, BUT WHEN I DID, I SAW DONNELLY HAD CLUTCHED BOTH OF THEM BY THE SCRUFFS OF THEIR NECKS AND WERE SLAMMING THEM AGAINST THE WALL."

WHEN HE SAW ME HE RAN OUTSIDE INTO THE GARDEN...

I RAN AFTER, BARKING AND HOWLING...

"...IN TIME TO SEE HIM SHOVE THEM INTO THE KILNS, LOCK THE DOORS, AND FIRE THEM UP."

ALL THE WHILE HE KEPT SHOUTING, "FIRE WILL CLEANSE YOU! BURN YOUR SINS AWAY! HALLELUJAH! HALLELUJAH!!"

EAMONN...
YOU WANTED TO KNOW, EVA.

"I SCREAMED... I HOWLED..."
"I EVEN TRIED TO ATTACK HIM BUT SOMEHOW HE'D GOTTEN HOLD OF A KNIFE AND KEPT ME AT BAY..."

"THE NEIGHBOURS WERE CALLING OVER THE WALL... SOME OF THEM HAD RUN INTO THE GARDEN..."
"THE CONFUSION GREW GREATER... AT LENGTH TWO OF THE NEIGHBOURS RUSHED ME OUT OF THE GARDEN AND INTO THEIR HOUSE."

I STRUGGLED...
I BEGGED EVERYBODY TO PLEASE, PLEASE SAVE MY BROTHERS...

WHEN I HEARD THEY WERE GONE...
...I RAN AWAY.

"I RAN FAR AWAY FROM WICKLOW... IN ANY DIRECTION... STEALING WHATEVER FOOD I COULD GET JUST TO SURVIVE BUT MOSTLY LIVING ON PURE ADRENALINE..."
"AND SUDDENLY I'D BECOME AWARE OF EVERYTHING... THAT I WAS TRULY THE ONE WHO KILLED SULLY AND NIALL... AND BOGS, WHO WAS SOMEHOW REAL TO ME... AND POSSIBLY DONNELLY TOO."
"AND ALL I'D WANTED TO DO WAS MAKE EVERYONE HAPPY."
"I COULDN'T TAKE IT. I EITHER WANTED TO DIE OR STOP KNOWING THIS. AND IN THE END... MAYBE OUT OF PURE SURVIVAL... I MANAGED TO ERASE IT ALL FROM MY MIND."
eire
CALLAGHAN & MURPHY
FRANK DOYLE
PURVEYORS OF FINE MEATS
OPEN

THINGS WERE...
... BETTER.
NOT GOOD.
JUST BETTER.

"NO MORE NIGHT-TIME FANTASIES...
MY DREAMS BECAME QUIETLY TRIVIAL."

44

... I'M SORRY, EAMONN.

I MEAN IT... I'M SORRY.

I DRIFTED INTO BECOMING A SERVICE ANIMAL BECAUSE I KNEW I HAD TO MAKE UP FOR SOMETHING.

"AND EVEN THEN I COULDN'T STAY FIXED... I EMIGRATED TO THE U.K., THEN AMERICA... AND THEN HIRO HAPPENED... NO MATTER WHAT, I COULD NEVER FIND ANY PEACE."

WHEN THE THREE OF YOU CAME ALONG, ALL THAT CHANGED. FINALLY, FINALLY, FINALLY... I COULD SET THINGS RIGHT.

AHEM... SO... SO WHEN...

... SO WHEN DID YOU FINALLY REMEMBER YOUR HISTORY WITH THE PROJECTION EDGE?
FROM THE MOMENT YOU STARTED, EVA, I KNEW IT WAS ALL VAGUELY FAMILIAR, BUT I COULDN'T PUT A POINT ON WHAT IT WAS ALL IN AID OF, UNTIL...

"HALLELUJAH."

... I'VE BEEN TRYING TO GET A HOLD OF YOU ...

FLUFFYPANTS!
WHAT'S GOING ON?!
YYYYEAH...

WHERE ARE YOU?
IN THE STORAGE AREA BENEATH THE STAIRWELL OF THE BASEMENT NEXT DOOR. BEST GAVE ME A KEY FOR EMERGENCIES.
EMERGENCIES?
YES. FOR INSTANCE, IN CASE FRIENDSTREAM DID AN END RUN AROUND BEST'S WISHES AND SENT ANIMAL CONTROL TO DO THEIR JACKBOOTED "RAUS-MACH-SCHNELL" ROUTINE ON US. WHICH, FUNNILY ENOUGH, IS EXACTLY WHAT HAPPENED.

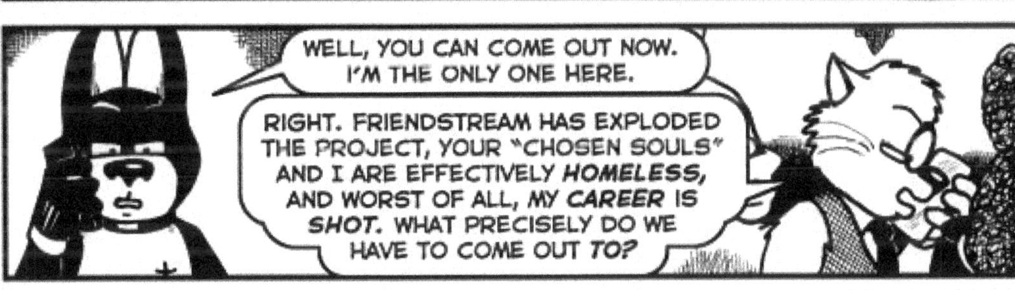

WELL, YOU CAN COME OUT NOW. I'M THE ONLY ONE HERE.
RIGHT. FRIENDSTREAM HAS EXPLODED THE PROJECT, YOUR "CHOSEN SOULS" AND I ARE EFFECTIVELY HOMELESS, AND WORST OF ALL, MY CAREER IS SHOT. WHAT PRECISELY DO WE HAVE TO COME OUT TO?

...GOD, I NEED A SMOKE.

TELL THE CHOSEN SOULS TO PREPARE FOR AN UPGRADE.

EAMONN...

I'M NOT PRETENDING I UNDERSTAND EVERYTHING THAT'S GOING ON. WHAT I'VE POSITED IS ONLY A THEORY. YOU DON'T KNOW WHAT PROBLEMS DONNELLY MIGHT HAVE BEEN HAVING.
STILL, I DON'T KNOW WHAT MIGHT HAVE HAPPENED IF I HADN'T BEEN SO RECKLESS.

I CAN'T HELP ANYONE WHO DOESN'T WANT TO BE HELPED. I KNOW THAT NOW.

...BUT THERE ARE SO MANY SAD, LONELY SOULS WHO MIGHT NEED US.

MARCEL, I'LL LISTEN TO YOU. PERHAPS THERE'S A WAY WE CAN DO THIS WITHOUT HARMING OTHERS.

PLEASE TELL ME WHAT YOU KNOW.

...IF ONLY WE COULD PERSUADE EAMONN THAT HE WASN'T TO BLAME AND HE DOESN'T NEED TO DO THIS.
HE WANTS TO HELP.

WHAT'S MARCEL GOING TO TELL EAMONN THAT'LL DO HIM ANY GOOD?

DO YOU REALLY THINK EAMONN'LL BE ABLE TO NEGOTIATE BRAIN CHEMICALS AS IF HE WERE SOLVING AN EXPLODING RUBIK'S CUBE?!
IF ANYONE COULD...

IF ANYONE COULD...

... LET ME TELL YOU SOMETHING.

WHEN I WAS A PUPPY, I DIDN'T HAVE A "BOGS" OR TAKE MY SIBLINGS ON TRIPS.
"I JUST LOOKED AT STARS AND GALAXIES AND UNDERSTOOD AMAZING THINGS ABOUT THEM."
"IT FELT LIKE THERE WAS NOTHING I COULDN'T LEARN."
"AS I GOT OLDER, I DISCOVERED THAT LEARNING TENDED TO GET MORE ABSTRACT, BUT I DIDN'T CARE."
"WHEN I HEARD ABOUT MIRANDA HAYES, I RAN AWAY FROM HOME AND BEGGED HER TO HELP ME REALIZE MY POTENTIAL."
"YOU COULD SAY I WAS ON A QUEST TO SEE, HEAR, FEEL, UNDERSTAND, AND INTERNALIZE MORE AND MORE KNOWLEDGE."
"I HOPED TO EVENTUALLY BECOME THE WISEST DOG IN THE WORLD..."
"AND ONCE I KNEW HOW TO CONTROL IT ALL, I WOULD SHARE WHAT I HAD FOUND."
LIKE A TEACHER.
LIKE A SAGE.
LIKE A BRIDGE.

AND THEN I FOUND EAMONN, WHO SEEMED MUCH MORE IN TUNE THAN I WAS, AND THE WORST MISTAKE I MAY HAVE EVER MADE WAS ASSUMING HE WANTED WHAT I WANTED, BECAUSE SERIOUSLY, WHO WOULDN'T WANT TO JUST... LEARN?!
YOU CAN STILL TEACH. NONE OF THIS IS STOPPING YOU.
I'M IN THIS UP TO MY NECK. DAMAGE CONTROL FROM SOMETHING I THOUGHT WOULD BENEFIT LIVING THINGS EVERY-WHERE. WISDOM IS EVIDENTLY JUST A GATEWAY DRUG TO DESTRUCTION.
I WAS NAIVE. AND NOW HERE WE ARE.
EAMONN'S WAY... OR NO WAY AT ALL.
COME ON, LET'S GO.
... IT'S CLEANUP TIME.

YOU MEAN WE CAN REALLY LIVE HERE?
YES, CHOSEN SOULS.

YOU HAVE EARNED IT. OUR MISSION WILL PROCEED AS ONE.
NOW... NOW REMEMBER...

THAT MEANS FOLLOWING RULES, YOU KNOW. THIS IS GIDEON BEST'S HOME, SO YOU HAVE TO BE ON YOUR BEST BEHAVIOR.
...SO TO SPEAK.
WE WILL!

BEHOLD... YOUR NEW HOME.
HALLELUJAH!

NOW GO UPSTAIRS TO THE ENTRY ROOM AND WAIT FOR ME THERE.
YES, REVEREND!

LISTEN, IS THIS PLACE ACTUALLY YOURS?!
I'M THE STEWARD FOR IT.
SO "NO," THEN.

HIS HEIRS HAVE PLANS TO MAKE THIS A MUSEUM, BUT THEY'RE TOO MESSED UP TO DO ANYTHING RIGHT NOW. SO I'M HERE TO KEEP THE PLACE INTACT, AND THEY'VE HIRED A CARETAKER TO HELP ME.
AH, AN ASSUREDLY TRUSTWORTHY THIRD PARTY. I'M SOLD.

THIS IS FLIRTING WITH DISASTER. IF ONE OF THOSE MANGY MONGRELS SO MUCH AS SLOBBERS ON A PILLOW, WE COULD ALL END UP ON DEATH ROW!
WHAT MADE BEST HIRE YOU, FLUFFYPANTS? YOUR TALENT FOR MAKING UP SHIT TO WORRY ABOUT?

...LOOK AT IT THIS WAY. WE WON'T HAVE TO WORRY ABOUT FRIENDSTREAM ANYMORE. WE CAN RECRUIT MORE CHOSEN SOULS WITH NO OVERSIGHT.
YOU PLAN TO BRING MORE DOGS HERE?!

...NOT NECESSARILY.

EVERY NIGHT... ANIMALS ON THE PERIPHERY... EITHER COWERING IN FEAR OR FROZEN IN PARALYZING CURIOSITY ABOUT THIS PLANE...
AND YET...
THERE ARE OTHERS PRESENT, WORKING HARD TO KEEP THINGS QUIET.
HA. IT SHOULD BE OBVIOUS THAT ANY ATTEMPT TO SILENCE THIS ONCOMING STORM WILL ONLY RESULT IN IT BECOMING LOUDER.
HEY! WAIT!
OH NO.
HOW CAN I GET YOU TO STOP FOLLOWING ME?
IF I HELP YOU FIND WHAT YOU'RE LOOKING FOR, WILL YOU HELP ME?
I AM HELPING YOU, YOU JUST—
BLAM!!

IT'S TOO LATE, GARRETT!! YOU BLEW IT! I'M BREAKING FREE!!

WHAT DID THAT MEAN?
IS IT NOT OBVIOUS?

IT'S TOO LATE TO DO ANYTHING MORE HERE. YOU NEED TO BREAK FREE FROM YOUR ADDICTIONS AND RESUME YOUR LIFE IN THE WAKING WORLD.
BUT MY WAKING WORLD IS --
-- EXACTLY WHAT YOU MAKE OF IT.
IF YOU UTILIZE ALL YOUR MENTAL ENERGIES HERE, YOU WILL "BLOW IT." YOU WILL DETERIORATE TO THE POINT WHERE YOU WON'T BE ABLE TO DO THIS AT ALL
STRAIGHTEN YOURSELF OUT IN THE WAKING WORLD FIRST, GARRETT. THEN MAYBE YOU CAN RETURN TO FIND ENLIGHTENMENT.

YOU'RE ASKING TOO MUCH OF ME. I CAN'T...
YOU CAN, BECAUSE IT MUST BE DONE. I BELIEVE YOU CAN DO IT. LET US SAY GOODBYE NOW.

I ... I HOPE YOU'RE RIGHT.
I HAVE FAITH IN YOU.

GOODBYE, GARRETT.

BOOM!!

WELL, MYSTERIOUS ENTITY, I'D THANK YOU FOR HELPING TO RID ME OF MY CODEPENDENT FRIEND...
RUMBLE RUMBLE
BLAM
RUMBLE RUMBLE
WHOOM
RUMBLE RUMBLE
BUT I BELIEVE YOU HAVE OTHER THINGS ON YOUR MIND RIGHT NOW.

HAS EAMONN ALREADY GONE TO BED?
YES, AND I'LL BE HEADING THERE MYSELF. IT'S BEEN A CRAZY DAY.
KNOCK KNOCK

HI, EVERYONE. SORRY TO DISTURB YOU SO LATE AT NIGHT...
THAT'S OKAY, GISELE. WHAT'S UP?

A BORDER COLLIE AND A TABBY KITTEN HAVE JUST SHOWN UP AT THE MAIN HOUSE AND THEY'RE ASKING FOR YOU...
WHAT?!! OMAGAW!

I CAN'T BELIEVE IT! I JUST CAN'T BELIEVE IT! BUDDY AND ARTHUR ARE REALLY HERE!!

HOW DID THEY KNOW WE WERE HERE?
BINGO.

RUMBLE
RUMBLE
RUMBLE
RUMBLE
RUMBLE
RUMBLE
RUMBLE
RUMBLE

RUMBLE RUMBLE RUMBLE RUMBLE RUMBLE
RUMBLE RUMBLE RUMBLE RUMBLE
EAMONN.
IT'S OVER.
AT LAST.
ROOOOOAR

I'M FREE.
CRASH

CHAPTER 11
"SHADOW OF
THE PAST"
I AGREED TO HELP THE FOUR OF YOU. I DID NOT AGREE TO START A PET HOTEL.
I PROMISE THEY WON'T BE HERE LONG.

BUT REALLY, THEY'RE TEST ANIMALS, AND CONSIDERING WHAT HAPPENED TO BIJOU, WE CAN AT LEAST OFFER THEM TEMPORARY SANCTUARY, CAN'T WE?
"...EMPHASIS ON 'TEMPORARY.'"
WE'LL WORK ON GETTING THEM A HOME, I SWEAR.

FINE. BUT NOT ONE MORE ANIMAL ENTERS MY HOUSE, DO YOU HEAR?

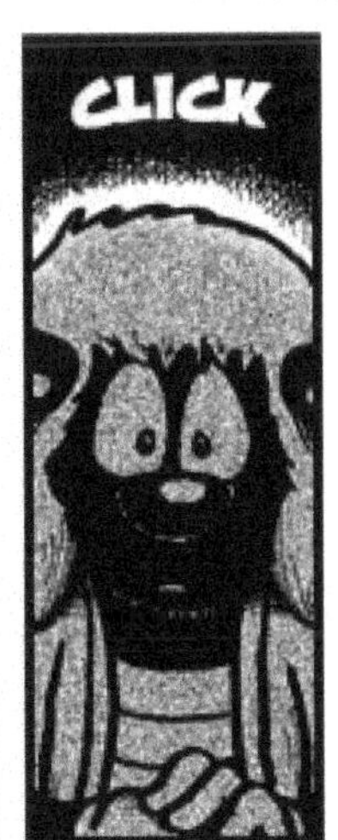

CLICK

WHAT DID SHE SAY?
WE'RE PROBABLY NOT GOING TO GET A SECOND TETHERBALL COURT.

BUT THEY CAN STAY?
FOR A SHORT WHILE, YES.

WHAT'S MORE IMPORTANT IS HOW THEY MANAGED TO FIND US. ONLY ADAM AND MIRANDA KNEW WHERE WE WERE GOING.
MAYBE THEY FOUND OUT FROM FRIENDSTREAM...?

I DUNNO. BIJOU, ARE BUDDY AND ARTHUR *JUST THAT AMAZING* AT DOXXING?
I DON'T THINK SO...

I MEAN, EVEN IF ADAM TOLD THEM I WAS NOW WITH SHELLEY, WHICH HE WOULDN'T... THE ONLY ELECTRONIC STUFF WE'RE ALLOWED TO TOUCH IS THE PS3 AND THE NINTENDO.
THOUGH SOMETIMES IF YOU ASK *SUPER* NICE, YOU CAN GET ON THE NET FOR AN HOUR.
" ...MAYBE HE ASKED *SUPERDUPER* NICE."

...IXNAY, HERE HE COMES.

HEY... UH... CAN YOU ALL C'MERE FOR A SEC?

...IS HE ALL RIGHT?

IT'S ... Y'KNOW ... THAT THING I WAS DOING WITH NELLIE.
"WHAT?"

ARE YOU STILL DOING THAT?
EAMONN... WAKE UP!

EVA!!

OH, LORD, I JUST—
SH!!

... AH. WELL. I GUESS I SHOULD GO TO SLEEP THEN, EH?

WOULD YOU MIND IF I SLEPT ON YOUR PORCH TONIGHT? I'VE GROWN TO LOVE SLEEPING OUTSIDE.

CLICK
WAS THAT... WHY IS HE HERE?
ONE THING AT A TIME. WHAT HAPPENED?

...BOGS.
"WHAT?"
...BOGS HAS RETURNED.

YOU MEAN THAT SEAGULL FRIEND YOU CREATED AS A PUPPY?!
I DIDN'T CREATE HIM. HE'S REAL. AND HE'S NOT WHAT I THOUGHT HE WAS.

WHAT IS HE?
I DON'T KNOW. I DON'T KNOW. I DON'T WANT TO KNOW!!

"CALM DOWN, EAMONN. ARTHUR'S ASLEEP IN THE NEXT ROOM."
"WAIT -- BOTH OF BIJOU'S FRIENDS ARE HERE? HOW?"

WE'LL HAVE TO TALK ABOUT THIS IN THE MORNING. LET'S STAY AWAY FROM THE PROJECTION EDGE FOR THE REST OF THE NIGHT. WE'LL SORT THIS OUT TOMORROW WHEN WE'RE FRESHER.

...RIGHT, SO.

THE NEXT MORNING...

I WENT OUT AT TWO, AND HE WAS STILL THERE...

BUT I LOOKED OUTSIDE AGAIN JUST NOW AND HE WAS GONE!
I'm sorry I had to leave, little Fella. Bijou and her friends will take good care of you. Don't worry, I'll be all right. — Buddy

WHY DID HE LEAVE? I DON'T GET IT!
I DON'T GET IT EITHER. HE COULDA AT LEAST STAYED THE NIGHT!
ARTHUR, DID BUDDY TELL YOU ANYTHING ELSE ABOUT YOUR LEAVING?

JUST THAT NEUROSMITH DIDN'T WANT US ANYMORE, AND THEY WERE GONNA GET RID OF US!
UH-HUH.

NOT A WORD ABOUT HOW HE KNEW WHERE WE WERE, OR HOW HE GOT THE MONEY TO TRAVEL THAT DISTANCE, OR EVEN WHY HE THOUGHT WE'D BE ABLE TO PUT YOU UP.
I'm sorry I had to leave, little Fella. you and her friends will good

...HE KEPT WHERE WE WERE GOING A SECRET.
ALL RIGHT, THAT'S IT. WHATEVER HAPPENS, TONIGHT IS GOING TO BE INTERESTING.

I SEE YOU'RE USING COASTERS. VERY GOOD.
OF COURSE! WE WANT TO BE GOOD EXAMPLES FOR THE NEW CHOSEN SOULS.

AH YES... WELL... LET'S HOPE WHEN THEY ARRIVE, THEY'RE AS CLEAN AS YOU ARE.
OH, THEY'RE NOT COMING HERE!

THE NEW CHOSEN SOULS ARE OUTSIDE THE GATES OF THE KINGDOM OF HEAVEN, WAITING TO BE LET IN!
THE KINGDOM... YOU MEAN, YOUR "DREAM WORLD?!"

"THAT'S RIGHT. ONCE WE'RE ASLEEP, THE REVEREND SAYS WE CAN CALL ALL THESE LOST SOULS TO HIM AND WE WILL ALL JOIN TOGETHER TO PLEASE GOD WITHIN THE KINGDOM OF HEAVEN!"

I THOUGHT I TOLD YOU, FLUFFYPANTS. CANINES EVERYWHERE ARE FINDING THEIR WAY TO THIS DREAMSCAPE ALREADY. YOU CAN FEEL THEM. THEY JUST NEED TO BE NUDGED IN OUR DIRECTION.

THIS IS MADNESS.
THE WORLD IS MADNESS. I'M THE ONE WHO'LL MAKE IT LOOK SANE.
riendstream
CENTRAL MOVING AND STORAGE

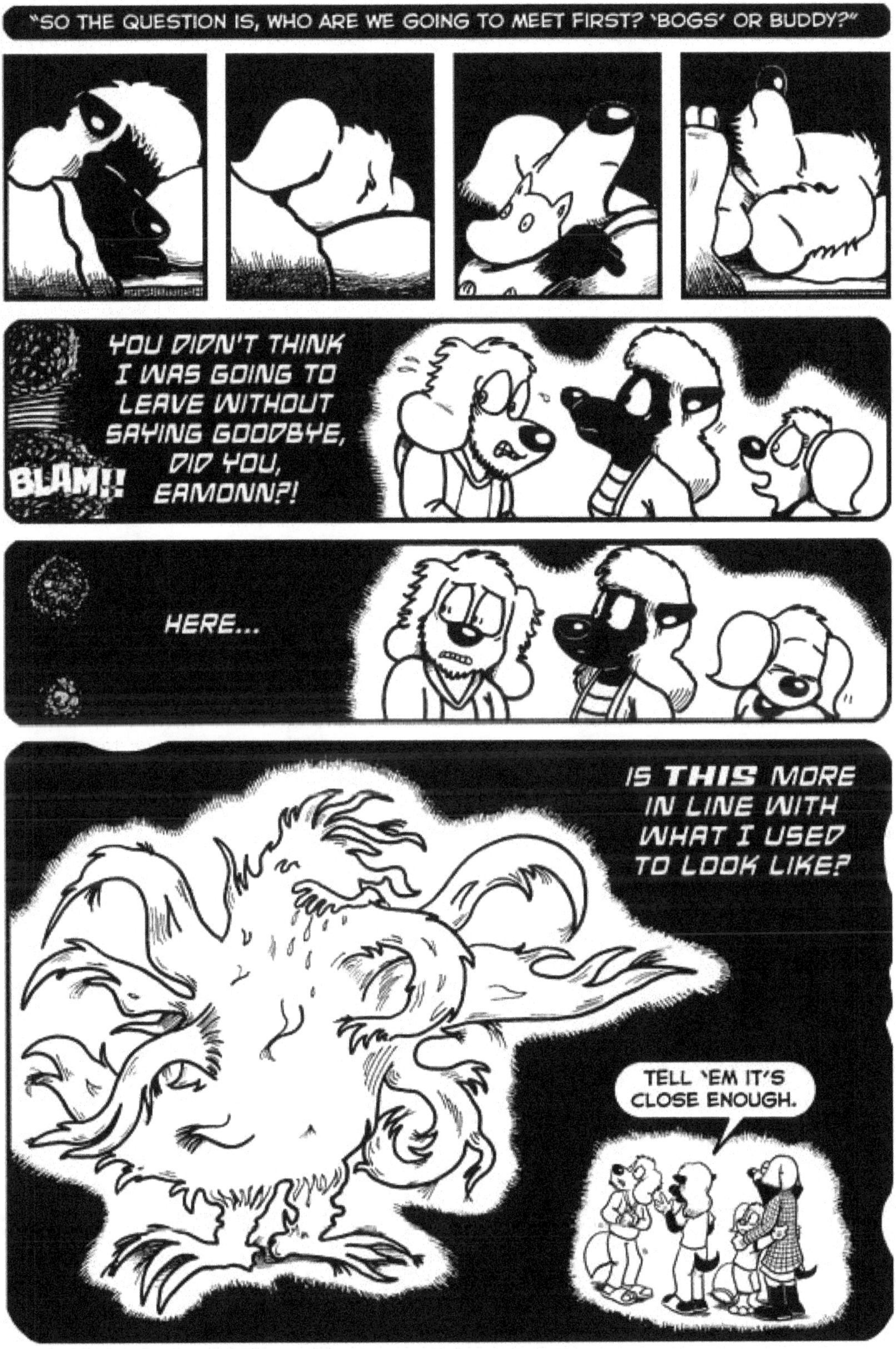

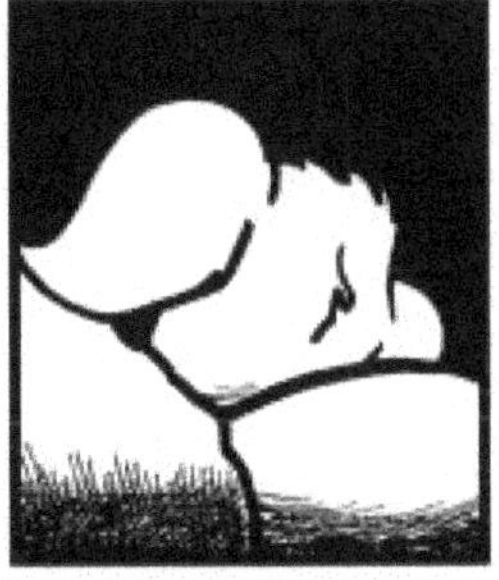

YOU DIDN'T THINK I WAS GOING TO LEAVE WITHOUT SAYING GOODBYE, DID YOU, EAMONN?!
BLAM!!
HERE...

IS THIS MORE IN LINE WITH WHAT I USED TO LOOK LIKE?
TELL 'EM IT'S CLOSE ENOUGH.

EVA. YOU DON'T HAVE TO PLAY SHY. WE'VE MET BEFORE, REMEMBER?
"YOU SHOULD HAVE BEEN THERE."
THAT WAS YOU?!

BEING A PRISONER MAKES ONE LESS COHERENT AND DECIDEDLY LESS EFFICIENT.
I TRIED TO HAVE BOTH YOU AND THAT "GARRETT" STOP EAMONN...
AND I FAILED.

YOU KNOW GARRETT TOO?!
...YOU ARE MUCH SLOWER THAN I EXPECTED, EVA.

WHO ARE YOU?! WHAT ARE YOU?!
HAVEN'T YOU MET BEINGS LIKE ME BEFORE?

NO.
ME NEITHER.
NOT ME.
SO EAMONN WAS THE LUCKY ONE, WAS HE?

I EXIST SEVERAL MILLION GALAXIES AWAY. I DON'T KNOW THE EXACT NUMBER. IT HARDLY MATTERS.

BACK BEFORE EAMONN HAD REACHED HIS MATURITY, HE WAS MY PLAYTHING.
HE'D SERVED ME WELL UNTIL THAT TOXIC HUMAN BLIGHTED OUR CONTACT. THAT'S HOW I BECAME A PRISONER.

HOW COULD YOU BE A PRISONER?!
GUESS WHAT, EAMONN. I DON'T KNOW. I ONLY KNOW YOU CAUSED IT.
... BACK UP.

YOU'RE ACTUALLY SAYING YOU'RE AN EXTRATERRESTRIAL.
...YOU REALLY ARE QUITE DENSE. MAYBE THAT'S WHY YOU NEVER LISTENED.

BIJOU... THIS IS INCREDIBLE.
TOTALLY.
ALL RIGHT, HOLD ON, HOLD ON, HOLD ON, HOLD ON...

SO WHAT I'M HEARING IS... YOU TOOK THE FORM OF A GIANT SEAGULL DURING EAMONN'S CONTACT WITH THE PROJECTION EDGE... BECAUSE YOU WERE USING HIM AS A TOY?!
IT HAS BEEN A TREND WITH US TO ACCESS THIS "EDGE," AS YOU CALL IT, TO TOY WITH BEINGS LIKE YOURSELVES FOR SOME TIME NOW.

GRANTED, MOST OF THESE GAMES ARE QUICKLY OVER. AS FOR MYSELF, I WAS BOTH BLESSED AND CURSED TO FIND THIS DANGEROUS THING.
I'M SO SORRY. I HONESTLY DID NOT MEAN FOR ANY OF THAT TO HAPPEN.

I REALIZE THAT. YOU WERE IMMATURE. ONE SHOULD NEVER TRUST CHILDREN. HOWEVER, I WON'T BE TAKING YOU TO CALIFORNIA OR WHATEVER THAT "GARDEN OF EDEN" WAS SUPPOSED TO BE ANYMORE.
GOODBYE, EAMONN.

WHERE ARE WE NOW, EAMONN?
WICKLOW.

IT'S WHERE I WANT TO BE RIGHT NOW. FAIR ENOUGH?
EAMONN...

TO PUT IT MILDLY... IT'S NOT EXPECTED THAT A PUPPY WOULD KNOW HOW TO HANDLE AN EXTRATERRESTRIAL WHO'S MESSING WITH YOU.

I CAN'T GET OVER THIS. WE'VE MADE CONTACT WITH ALIEN INTELLIGENCE.
YEAH...

EVA, YOU WERE RIGHT. THIS IS WAY BIGGER THAN WE THOUGHT IT WAS.
YES, I'M SORRY IF WE EVER DISMISSED WHAT YOU WERE TELLING US.

...TO TELL THE TRUTH, I'M NOT SURE IF I'M ABLE TO DEAL WITH THIS MYSELF.
"UH... HELLO?"

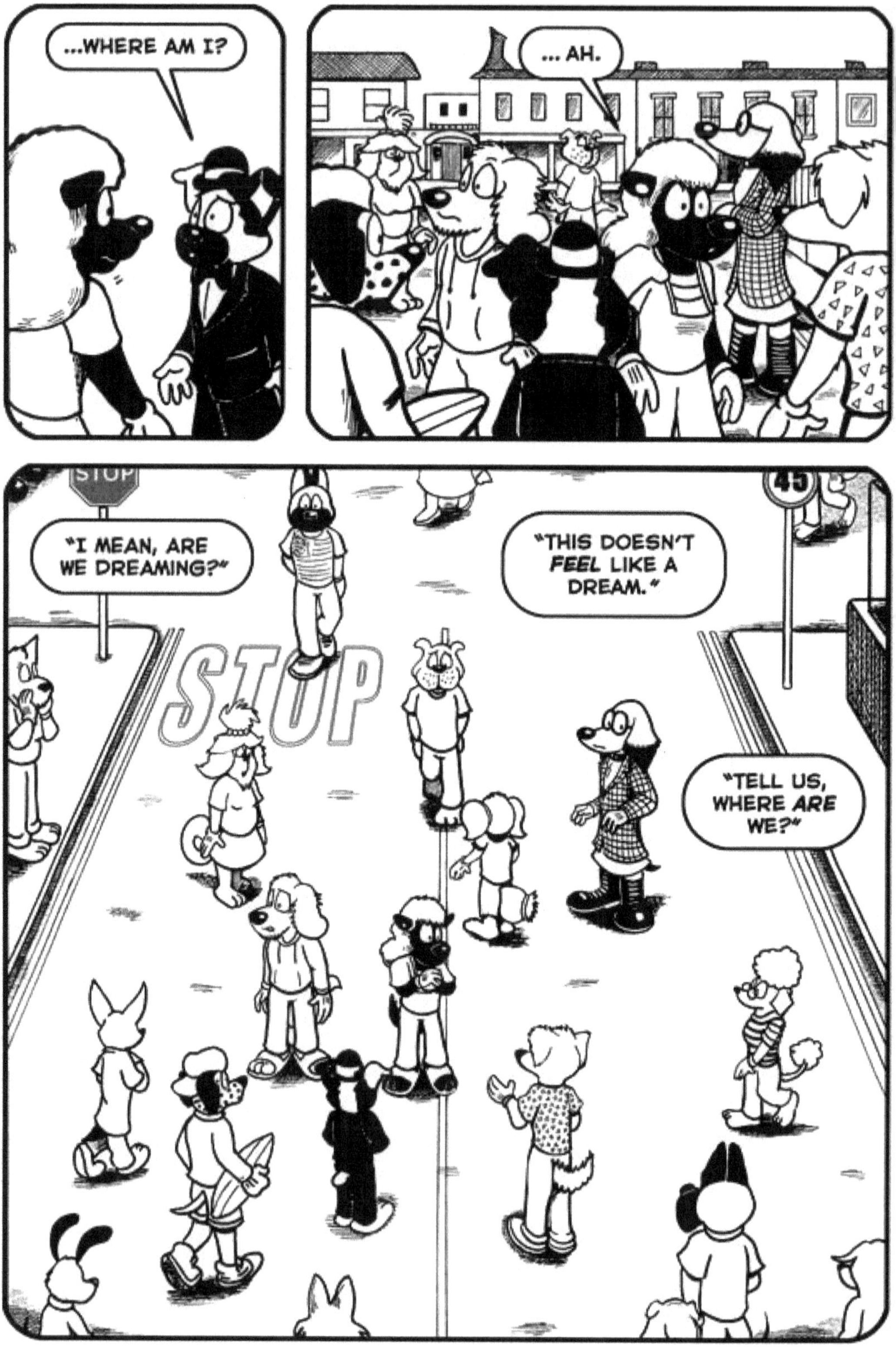

...WHERE AM I?

... AH.

"I MEAN, ARE WE DREAMING?"
STOP
"THIS DOESN'T FEEL LIKE A DREAM."
"TELL US, WHERE ARE WE?"

WHO ARE THEY? HOW DID THEY GET HERE SO FAST?
GREAT QUESTIONS. I'LL SAVE THEM FOR LATER.

EVERYBODY, LISTEN UP!!

"THIS IS NOT A DREAM... WELL, NOT EXACTLY..."

ALL OF YOU HAVE... RATHER SUDDENLY... BROKEN FREE OF YOUR FEARS AND ARE NOW ACCESSING WHAT WE CALL THE PROJECTION EDGE!

... SHE KNOWS!!
THE WHAT?!

GOOD LORD, WHERE TO BEGIN...

...DAMMIT!!!

"WHAT'S HAPPENING?!"
"DAMMIT" INDEED...

"WELL DONE."
THEY'LL FORGET. OR IT'LL BE HAZY.

... OR AT LEAST THEY'LL BE ABLE TO CONVINCE THEMSELVES IT WAS ALL A DREAM. THIS ONE WAS ROUGH.

I KNOW.
IT APPEARS WE'LL HAVE TO DEAL WITH EAMONN ON TOP OF OUR OTHER PROBLEM.

I GUESS SO. THE DIFFERENCE IS HE'S... GOOD-HEARTED.
TRULY THE MOST ALTRUISTIC TORNADO IN THE WORLD.

HONESTLY, I THOUGHT BIJOU WAS JUST PLAYING. SHE DESERVED TO HAVE SOME FUN IN HER LIFE.
IT'S IN THE PAST. BUT IT SHOWS YOU CAN'T LET UP FOR EVEN A SECOND.

I COULDN'T STAY TO WORK ON THEM, THOUGH. PRUDENCE IS STILL BEING... PRUDENCE.
WE'LL HELP YOU WITH EAMONN. WE ALL WILL. YOU CAN'T DO THIS ALONE.
MAYBE WITH HIS "OTHER" COMPANION FROM HIS YOUTH GONE FOR GOOD, HIS FIRE WILL ABATE.
THIS BRINGS US TO OUR CURRENT ISSUE...

YOU'LL HAVE TO HELP US WITH OUR "OTHER."

IT HASN'T DONE A THING TO STOP THE REVEREND SINCE THE REVEREND FIRST SHOWED UP.

WHAT?! HOW CAN I HELP YOU? I'VE GOT ENOUGH ON MY PLATE!
IF YOU CAN HANDLE LA SALLE, YOU CAN HANDLE THIS.

I CAN'T DO IT! FREE ME! I CAN'T PUT OUT ITS FIRE!!
YOU CERTAINLY CAN, YOU INSOLENT BRUTE!

YOU HAVE TO FREE ME FIRST!!
NOT UNTIL YOU'VE CUT THE REVEREND OFF!
MAYBE THIS IS TOO MUCH FOR IT...

MAYBE IT'S TOO MUCH FOR ALL OF US... MAYBE THIS IS THE MOMENT WE'RE ALL IN OVER OUR HEADS...

WHACK
"AFTER ALL THAT..."

I DON'T KNOW WHAT I COULD POSSIBLY SAY TO CONVINCE YOU THAT WE'RE DEALING WITH SOMETHING SO MUCH LARGER THAN OURSELVES, AND MUCH MORE DANGEROUS.

SOMETHING YOU DID HAS OPENED THE DOOR TO ANY NUMBER OF UNPREPARED DOGS, AND NOW THEIR SLEEP WILL BE STEEPED IN CONFUSION THAT WILL SPILL OVER INTO THEIR WAKING LIFE.
PLUCK

AND ALL OF THEM COULD POTENTIALLY BE MANIPULATED BY THOSE PREVIOUSLY UNKNOWN FORMS OF INTELLIGENCE, WHATEVER THEY ARE.
EVA...

IF I TOLD YOU MY NEED TO MAKE THINGS BETTER WAS NOT JUST A SELFISH DESIRE, BUT CAME PARTLY FROM... THE PROJECTION EDGE ITSELF... WOULD YOU BELIEVE ME?

YES.

BUT THAT DOESN'T ABSOLVE ANY OF US OF RESPONSIBILITY FOR OUR FUTURE ACTIONS.

"THAT'S WHY OUR APPROACH WILL BE 'SLOW DOWN AND BE CAREFUL.' NOT A *SEXY* MESSAGE, NO, BUT ONE THAT SEVERAL NERVOUS ANIMALS MIGHT BE RECEPTIVE TO."

YOU KNOW, WE STILL DON'T KNOW IF BUDDY'S SEEN THE PROJECTION EDGE.
OH, HE HAS.

WE DIDN'T SEE HIM... BUT FOR THE FIRST TIME I SENSED HE WAS WATCHING US FROM SOMEWHERE.

DOES THAT MEAN THAT SOMEHOW BUDDY WAS DOING WHAT YOU GUYS ARE DOING?
YA.
THAT'S KINDA SCARIER THAN I THOUGHT IT WOULD BE.

THANKS A LOT FOR PICKING ME UP! I KNOW IT CAN'T HAVE BEEN EASY DRIVING ALL THAT WAY.
WELL, YA KNOW... WHEN THE CEO OF THE COMPANY YOU WORK FOR ASKS YOU TO DO SOMETHING, YOU'D BE AN IDIOT NOT TO DO IT.

REMEMBER, CHOSEN SOULS! THEY'RE OUT ON THE FRINGES! THEY'RE OUT IN THE CORNERS!
SEEK THESE LOST ONES OUT AND LEAD THEM TO THE KINGDOM OF HEAVEN, TO THE GREATEST REWARD OF ALL!

LOOK! THE REVEREND WAS RIGHT!

AH, HELLO... LAST NIGHT I WAS IN SOME STRANGE TOWN... YOU WOULDN'T HAPPEN TO KNOW WHERE I AM NOW, WOULD YOU?

YOU'RE ON THE WAY TO HEAVEN!!!
WHAT?

THAT'S RIGHT! WE'RE HERE TO HELP YOU GET THERE AND BECOME ONE WITH GOD!
REALLY?

WELL, THAT'S NICE, BUT...

BLAM!

...OKAY, I'D RATHER NOT BE ALONE.
HALLELUJAH!

CCC

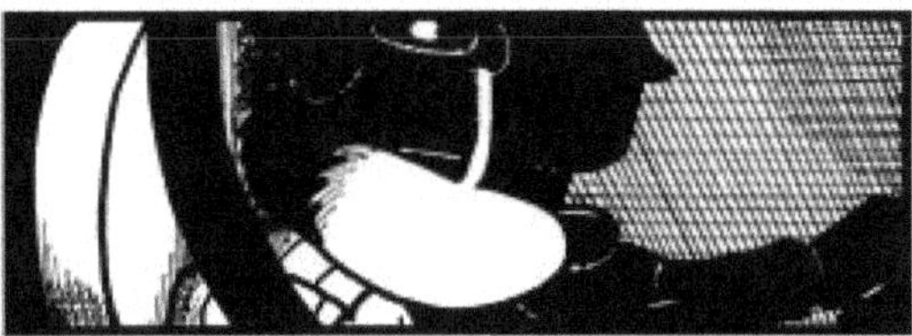

RECTORY AND CAFE
HELLO, MS. LA SALLE!

IT LOOKS LIKE I'LL BE THERE AROUND 5:30 IN THE MORNING.
IS THAT RIGHT?
"YOU WILL FIND A WAY TO LET ME IN QUIETLY AND SECRETLY, WON'T YOU?"
YOU...
YOU...

... YOU'VE BEEN ORDERING ME AROUND QUITE A BIT THESE LAST FEW MONTHS.
OH COME NOW...

IT'S WHAT YOU WANT TO DO.
IT'S PART OF OUR SHARED GOAL TO ENSURE US ANIMALS STAY IN OUR PLACE.

BUT I DON'T FEEL LIKE YOU'RE STAYING IN YOUR PLACE. I FEEL LIKE YOU'RE USING ME.
TRUST ME, MS. LA SALLE. I WANT WHAT YOU WANT.

...PLEASE FIND A WAY TO LET ME IN AT 5:30 AM.
DISCREETLY.

CRASH!

REVEREND!

REVEREND, WE HAVE A NEW CHOSEN...
WHOA.
DID YOU DO THIS?
WELL WELL.

HOW DID YOU GET HERE?
I DON'T KNOW!

WHEN I WAS HERE LAST TIME IT WAS SOME EUROPEAN-LOOKING TOWN, AND NOW IT'S GONE!

I MEAN, I'M NOT ACTUALLY DREAMING, AM I?
OF COURSE NOT.

YOUR WAKING LIFE IS THE DREAM.
THIS IS THE REALITY.

THE REALITY OF HEAVEN. AND WE ARE GOING TO MAKE IT OURS.
WOW, WHAT'S THIS?
THE REVEREND MADE IT!

MARINA BELLA, CALIFORNIA
CCC
WHIRR
CLICK

YOU MUST BE LA SALLE'S FRIEND.
YES!

I'VE GOT YOUR VISITOR'S BADGE, JUST LIKE SHE REQUESTED. I'LL LEAD YOU TO YOUR OFFICE.

CCC

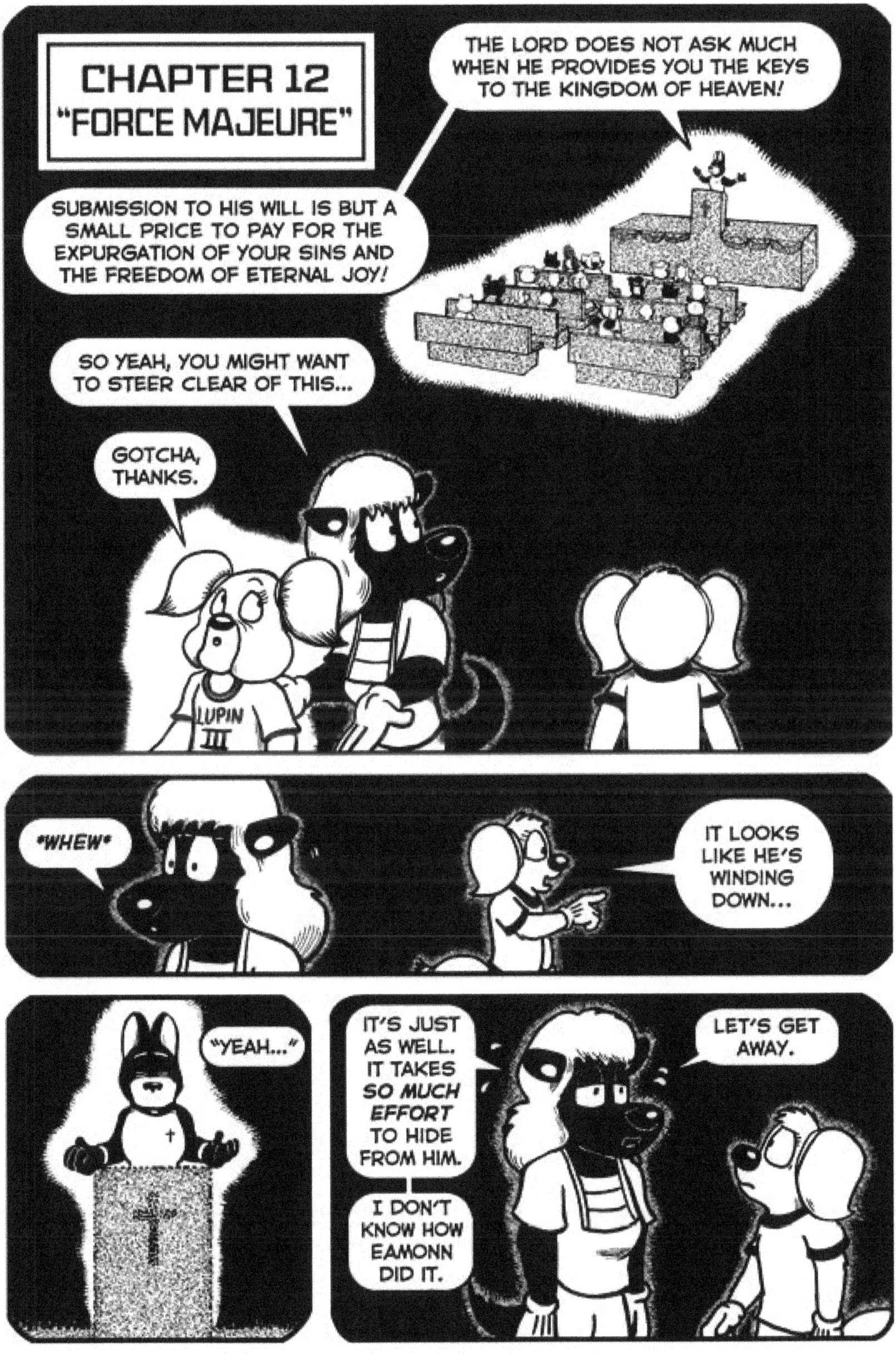

THE LORD DOES NOT ASK MUCH WHEN HE PROVIDES YOU THE KEYS TO THE KINGDOM OF HEAVEN!
SUBMISSION TO HIS WILL IS BUT A SMALL PRICE TO PAY FOR THE EXPURGATION OF YOUR SINS AND THE FREEDOM OF ETERNAL JOY!
SO YEAH, YOU MIGHT WANT TO STEER CLEAR OF THIS...
GOTCHA, THANKS.
LUPIN III

WHEW
IT LOOKS LIKE HE'S WINDING DOWN...

"YEAH..."

IT'S JUST AS WELL. IT TAKES SO MUCH EFFORT TO HIDE FROM HIM.
I DON'T KNOW HOW EAMONN DID IT.
LET'S GET AWAY.

I DON'T LIKE WHAT'S HAPPENING HERE...
IT'S NOT PARTICULARLY FUN, IS IT?

QUENBY DIDN'T TELL US JUST HOW *MAGNETIC* THIS "REVEREND" GUY IS.

I DON'T KNOW HOW OR IF WE CAN EVEN BREAK THIS UP...
EVA...

EAMONN AND I FOUND ANOTHER COUPLE OF DOGS. WE WERE ABLE TO CALM THEM DOWN UNTIL THEY WOKE UP...
IT'S GETTING TO BE TOO MANY ...

I KNOW... AND THOSE ARE JUST THE ONES WE CAN *SEE*...

'SCUSE ME, MA'AM?
GRK!

!

I DON'T KNOW WHAT YOU MEAN.
ROOM 307 ON THE THIRD FLOOR.
THE ONE THAT CAWTHORN USED TO OCCUPY.
IT'S BEING OCCUPIED AGAIN... BY A DOG.

...A DOG.
"A BORDER COLLIE."

"DRESSED QUITE CASUALLY."
"WHEN ANYONE APPROACHES HIM, HE SHRUGS AND TELLS PEOPLE TO ASK YOU ABOUT IT."
"HE'S BEEN THERE FOR WEEKS."

I DON'T KNOW WHAT YOU'RE TALKING ABOUT.
COME SEE.
HE'S THERE NOW.

I DON'T HAVE TIME FOR THIS. I HAVE A MEETING. IF THERE'S SOME STRANGE DOG SQUATTING IN ONE OF OUR OFFICES, TALK TO SECURITY, NOT ME. I HAVE BETTER THINGS TO DO.
WE... HAVE... TALKED TO SECURITY.

I CAN'T DO ANYTHING ABOUT HIM. HE ANSWERS TO LA SALLE. YOU'LL HAVE TO TALK TO HER.
SECUR

Y'KNOW, DESPITE ALL THE DOGS WE'VE FOUND, WE STILL HAVEN'T SEEN BUDDY.

HE'S STILL HIDING.

AND CONSIDERING HOW DIFFICULT IT IS TO "HIDE," I CAN'T IMAGINE HOW HE'S BEEN ABLE TO KEEP IT UP.

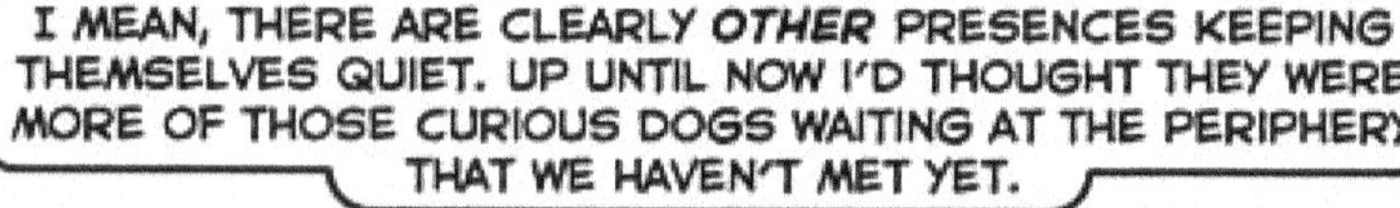

IT'S FAR EASIER ONCE YOU'RE USED TO IT.
APPARENTLY.

I MEAN, THERE ARE CLEARLY OTHER PRESENCES KEEPING THEMSELVES QUIET. UP UNTIL NOW I'D THOUGHT THEY WERE MORE OF THOSE CURIOUS DOGS WAITING AT THE PERIPHERY THAT WE HAVEN'T MET YET.

WHAT DOES THAT MEAN?
I DON'T KNOW.

OBVIOUSLY BUDDY HAS SOME ANGLE ON THE PROJECTION EDGE THAT WE DON'T, AND HE'S DOING EVERYTHING HE CAN TO KEEP IT FROM US.

...I NEVER THOUGHT I'D LIKE CATS.

SKRITCH SKRITCH SKRITCH
PURR PURR
PURR PURR
PURR PURR

ALL THIS NONSENSE ABOUT A DOG SQUATTING IN OUR OFFICES. MADNESS.
I'LL JUST PROVE THAT—
CLICK
KEEP THIS DOOR LOCKED.

...YOU'VE SEEN THE REVEREND, AND THE ONES HE'S TALKING TO. YOU JUST HAVE TO DISCREDIT HIM LOUDLY IN FRONT OF HIS AUDIENCE.
...AND THEN I CAN GO?

FIRST WE HAVE TO SEE IF IT WORKS. HE HAS AN ABILITY TO SPIN THINGS TO HIS ADVANTAGE.
YOU'LL NEVER LET ME GO. IT'LL BE ONE EXCUSE AFTER ANOTHER.

LOOK, YOU'RE COHERENT NOW. JUST INTERRUPT HIS SERMON WITH... I DON'T KNOW... A STATEMENT THAT HE'S FOUL IN THE EYES OF GOD, PERHAPS.
I DON'T KNOW WHAT THAT MEANS.

DENOUNCE HIM. DEPRECATE HIM. YELL OUT THAT HE'S MISLEADING EVERYBODY. THAT'S ALL WE ASK.
I THINK I UNDERSTAND. I WILL TRY.

PLEASE DON'T BE MISLEADING ME.

BEATRICE DUNCAN ... NELLIE DUNCAN'S MOTHER ...
Personal

WHAT THE HELL IS GOING ON IN HERE?!
I'M JUST RELAXING...

BUT IF IT'S OKAY, I THINK I WANT TO TAKE A WALK OUTSIDE NOW.

I ASKED HER FOR THIS...
BUT WHY?
AND WHY HAVEN'T I OPENED IT?
SHE SENT THIS OVER TWO WEEKS AGO AFTER I ASKED FOR IT...
AND I HID IT IN A FILING CABINET?!

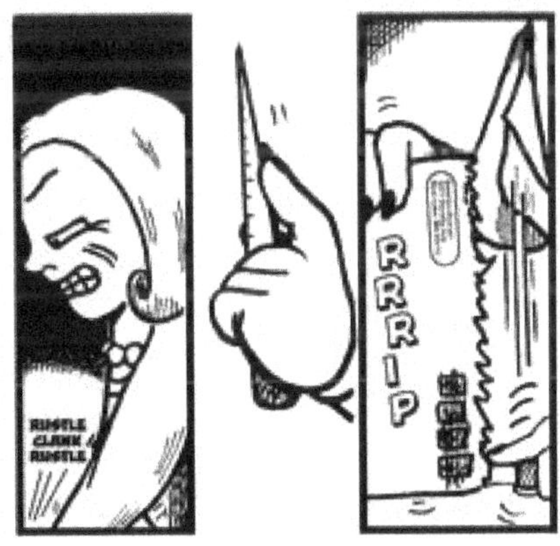

RUSTLE CLINK RUSTLE
RRRIP

HELL NO. THERE'S SOMETHING STRANGE ABOUT ALL THIS. LA SALLE TOLD ME TO KEEP THIS OFFICE DOOR LOCKED... AND YOU'RE STAYING HERE.

WAIT...

...WHAT IS IT?

"NEVER MIND."

NOW I KNOW.

NELLIE DUNCAN. THAT'S RIGHT.
I FINANCED HER ANIMAL SUBMISSION PROJECT. BECAUSE THE SUBSERVIENCE OF THE UNCLEAN IS THE WILL OF GOD. SHE WAS SUPPOSEDLY MAKING PROGRESS UNTIL SHE... BECAME ILL... SOMEHOW.

I'M DEACTIVATING YOUR BADGE. NOT ONLY WILL YOU NOT BE ABLE TO LEAVE THE BUILDING, WE'LL KNOW IF YOU TRY.

SO WHY IS THIS DOG... HERE?!

YES, BUDDY WAS NELLIE'S TEST ANIMAL ORIGINALLY. I SUPPOSE IT COULD HAVE BEEN THE SAME PROJECT, BUT I WASN'T INVOLVED THEN. NELLIE HAD JUST BEEN MOVED FROM YUBA CITY AFTER HER FAILURE WITH THAT COLLIE DOG FROM MEGANEWSWEST.

IS THERE ANY WAY TO FIND OUT?
THEY'VE LOCKED DOWN EVERYTHING NELLIE EVER WORKED ON.
SO NO.

ARE YOU SURE, ADAM?
"LISTEN..."
I CAN'T DEAL WITH THIS RIGHT NOW.

"I'VE GOT BIGGER PROBLEMS OF MY OWN."
WHAT DO YOU MEAN?

...I SUPPOSE YOU SHOULD KNOW. I SEEM TO BE HAVING MEMORY LAPSES THESE DAYS.

WHAT SORT OF MEMORY LAPSES?

... FOR STARTERS, APPARENTLY I WITHDREW $300 FROM OUR BANK ACCOUNT AND HAVE NO IDEA WHAT I DID WITH IT.

WE THOUGHT IT WAS FRAUD... UNTIL THE BANK TOLD US I WAS CAUGHT ON CAMERA. MY WIFE WASN'T TOO HAPPY ABOUT THAT.
SURPRISE, SURPRISE, SURPRISE!

"HAVE YOU TALKED TO YOUR DOCTOR?"
...HE SAID IT WAS STRESS, BUT AFTER I BEGGED AND PLEADED HARD, A SPECIALIST ORDERED CAT SCANS. WHICH TURNED OUT TO BE INCONCLUSIVE.
WHERE THE HELL ARE YA? WHERE THE HELL ARE YA, SIMON?!

THIS HAS REALLY STRAINED MY MARRIAGE, AND I'M NOW BEGINNING TO WORRY WHAT ELSE MIGHT BE HAPPENING TO ME.

CLICK CLICK SQUEEEK
...LOOK, I GOTTA GO.

"IF I FIND OUT ANYTHING ABOUT BUDDY, I'LL LET YOU KNOW. GOODBYE."
BEEEP

WHOOSH

SORRY TO DISTURB YOU, SHELLEY, BUT WE NEED TO TALK TO ARTHUR FOR A BIT.

CAN WE TALK?
SURE.

ONE OF YOUR "CHOSEN SOULS" HAS INFORMED ME THAT YOUR "DREAMLAND CONGREGATION" HAS EXPANDED TO TWENTY-SIX.
THIRTY-ONE. THEY REALLY CAN'T COUNT.

WHY AM I HEARING THIS STUFF FROM THE RUBES AND NOT YOU?
YOU'RE NEVER INTERESTED. THE LAST TIME I TOLD YOU SOMETHING IMPORTANT YOU SHOUTED "THIS IS MADNESS" AND HUNG UP THE PHONE.

I'M NOT SOME MINDLESS FACTOTUM, YOU KNOW. I WOULD LIKE TO KNOW WHAT SORT OF SANCTIFIED BEDLAM IT IS THAT I'M ENABLING.
FLUFFYPANTS...

HAVE YOU CONSIDERED JOINING US?

... W-WHAT?

NO ONE'S EVER SAID THIS WAS EXCLUSIVE TO DOGS.

...THAT'S WHAT I THOUGHT.

BUDDY TOLD ME HE'D ACTUALLY *SAVED* THE MONEY!
NO ONE THERE *EVER* GIVES US MONEY, ARTHUR.

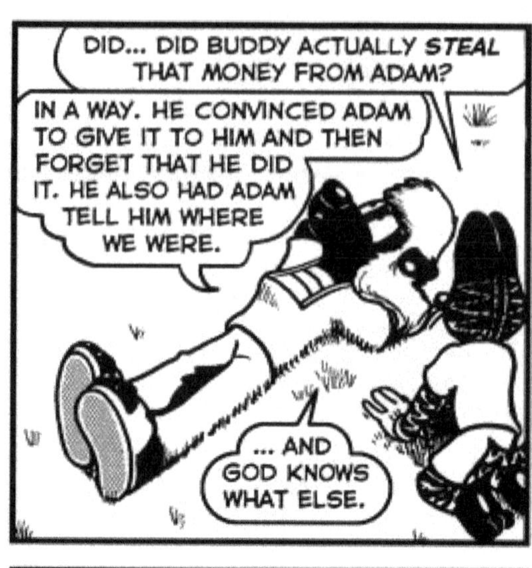

DID... DID BUDDY ACTUALLY *STEAL* THAT MONEY FROM ADAM?
IN A WAY. HE CONVINCED ADAM TO GIVE IT TO HIM AND THEN FORGET THAT HE DID IT. HE ALSO HAD ADAM TELL HIM WHERE WE WERE.
... AND GOD KNOWS WHAT ELSE.

I THINK WE *ALL* KNOW WHERE AND WHEN WE'RE ABLE TO MAKE HUMANS HYPER-SUSCEPTIBLE TO *SUGGESTION*.

THAT DOESN'T SOUND LIKE THE BUDDY I KNOW!
ME NEITHER... BUT SHE'S RIGHT.

SO! WE'RE NOT ALONE IN BEING ABLE TO MANIPULATE MINDS AND EMOTIONS. AND MAYBE AS WE SHOULD'VE PREDICTED, *SOME* AREN'T USING THIS IN AS BENEVOLENT A WAY AS *WE'VE* BEEN.

CAN WE MAKE ANY GUESSES AS TO HOW, SAY, THE *REVEREND* MIGHT FIND AN ABILITY LIKE THIS *USEFUL?*

WE HAVE TO STOP THE REVEREND NOW.
HOW CAN WE?

HE'S VERY STRONG-WILLED. EVEN IF WE ALL BARGED IN AND MADE SOME DRAMATIC SCENE, I DON'T THINK THAT WOULD SWAY A SINGLE MIND.
I MEAN, WHEN HE QUESTIONED ME...IF I'D STAYED ANY LONGER, I WOULD HAVE TOLD HIM ANYTHING.

EVEN THOUGH THERE WAS NOTHING TO TELL! I WOULD HAVE MADE IT UP! HE WAS JUST THAT PERSUASIVE!
IT'S TRUE HE HAS SOME KIND OF GRIP ON HIS FOLLOWERS...

...BUT I THINK EVERYBODY'S FORGETTING SOMETHING.
"'EAMONN THE FIRE GOD' HASN'T SPOKEN TO THE FAITHFUL YET."

WHAT -- HOW CAN YOU SAY THAT?!
LISTEN TO ME. IT'S THE ONLY WAY WE'LL HAVE ANY IMPACT.

I'M NOT SAYING YOU SHOULD MAKE THUNDEROUS PRONOUNCEMENTS.
TELL THE TRUTH.

THE REVEREND DOESN'T KNOW WHAT HE'S DOING AND ALL OF THEIR LIVES COULD BE AT RISK. VERY SIMPLE.

I MEAN, YOU DON'T HAVE TO TELL THEM ABOUT THE ALIENS, WE DON'T WANT TO START A PANIC...
LET ME SET THIS STRAIGHT...

I DON'T LIKE THAT PART OF ME. IT KILLED MY BROTHERS, DONNELLY AND POSSIBLY NELLIE.
WE DON'T KNOW—

NO. NEVER AGAIN.
NEVER AGAIN.

IT WASN'T A GOOD IDEA ANYWAY.
FINE. WE DO THIS WITHOUT "DIVINE INTERVENTION."
WHO IS THIS "REVEREND?"
I'LL EXPLAIN LATER.

("AREN'T YOU TAKING TOO MANY AFTERNOON NAPS?" "I FIND THEM VERY REFRESHING.")

"HIS 'CHURCH' IS BIGGER NOW."
"YES, I THINK HE'S QUICKLY FIGURING ALL OF THIS OUT."

...SO NOW'S THE TIME.
DEFO FOR SURE.
...CAN I JUST SEE HOW THIS GOES?

YOU'RE GOOD, QUENBY. EVA 'N' I CAN HANDLE THIS.
OKAY, LET'S GET GOING. ON MY SIGNAL.... WE BOTH STOP HIDING.

...AND YET! THE KING OF HEAVEN IS JUST AS LIKELY TO BE AN ANGRY GOD!!
the border collie said to denounce the reverend...
deprecate him...
yell out that he's misleading everybody...
how do i do that?
i don't even understand what he's saying...

i don't know what's going on...
...but i have to do this right or they won't let me go...

CAN WE REALLY STAY HIDDEN WHILE WE'RE NEXT TO THEM?
EVEN IF WE CAN'T...

...i can't think...
...i can't focus...
...but i have to put out his fire...

... IT WON'T MATTER.

...i want to be free...
...how am i going to do this...

...BECAUSE HERE WE GO.

EVERYBODY! PAY ATTENTION AND LISTEN TO ME!

YOU ARE ALL IN DANGER! YOU HAVE TO LEAVE NOW!

...WHO ARE YOU?! WHERE DID YOU COME FROM? WHAT DO YOU MEAN?!
YOU LISTEN TOO, REVEREND.

what is happening...
... i have to stop this ...
"THIS APPLIES TO YOU AS MUCH AS ANYBODY."
"WHAT?!"

LISTEN TO ME. THIS "WORLD" YOU'RE IN IS UNPREDICTABLE AND COULD BE VERY DANGEROUS TO YOUR WAKING SELVES IF YOU'RE NOT CAREFUL!
ANSWER ME!! WHO ARE YOU?

I'M THE ONE TELLING YOU THAT YOU HAVE TO LEAVE! YOU HAVE TO KNOW MORE BEFORE YOU CAN--
AND I'M THE ONE TELLING YOU THAT IT'S YOU WHO HAS TO LEAVE!

now

BOOM

DON'T LISTEN TO THIS!
THIS IS BAD!!
I DENOUNCE THIS COMPLETELY!
BLAM
CRASH

THWOOM

WHAT'S GOING ON?!
OHHH-KAY...
"ISN'T IT OBVIOUS?!"

THE KING OF HEAVEN IS ANGERED BY THE INTRUDER! WE MUST GET HER OUT OF HERE BEFORE SHE DOOMS US ALL!!

YOU HEARD HIM! GET OUT!!
NOW WAIT--
HUH?!

RUMBLE RUMBLE RUMBLE RUMBLE

RUMBLERUMBLERUMBLE
RUMBLE
RUMBLE
RUMBLE
RUMBLERUMBL
RUMBLE
RUMBLE
RUMBLERUMBLE
RUMBLERUMBLE

LET THEM GO.
LET THEM ALL
GO.

... I'M SORRY, WERE YOU TALKING TO ME?

... WHATEVER. GO TO HELL. OR, IF YOU PREFER...

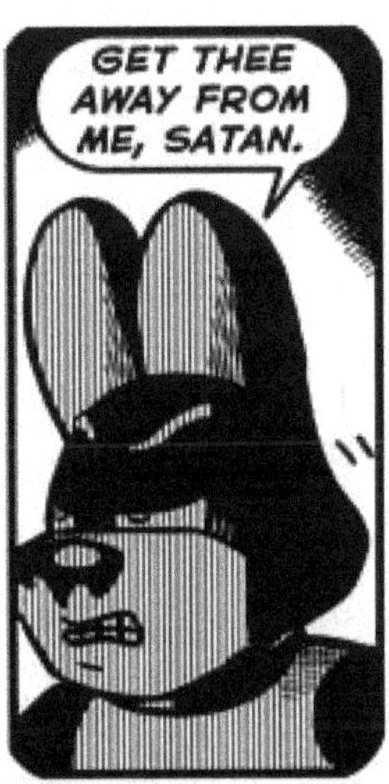
GET THEE AWAY FROM ME, SATAN.

RUMBLE RUMBLE RUMBLE RUMBLE
RUMBLE RUMBLE RUMBLE
RUMBLERUMBLERUMBLE
RUMBLERUMBLE
RUMBLERUMBLE
RUMBLERUMBLE
RUMBLE RUMBLE
RUMBLE
RUMBLE
RUMBLE
RUMBLE

IT'S SATAN! IT'S SATAN! YOU BROUGHT HIM HERE!!
WHAT?! NO!
GET HER!!
RUMBLE RUMBLE RUMBLEmmmm

P O W
BIJOU!! ARE YOU ALL RIGHT?!
BIJOU!!!

GRRR...
WHINE

GRRRR...
ARRRGH...
SNX
GRRRR....

WAKE UP!

CAN'T YOU SEE WHAT YOU'RE DOING?!

AREN'T YOU EVEN AWARE?!!

I WAS WRONG ...
SHE MAY NEED TO FIND OUT WHAT I KNOW ...

WAS IT REALLY SATAN?!
IT SURE AIN'T WHAT I THOUGHT SATAN'D LOOK LIKE.
THE PRINCE OF DARKNESS CAN ASSUME ANY SHAPE HE PLEASES!

THIS IS HOW HE WILL TRY TO TAKE THE KINGDOM OF HEAVEN AWAY FROM US! WE HAVE DISCOVERED OUR FIGHT WILL NOT BE EASY! ALREADY SOME HAVE RUN IN FEAR, BUT THIS IS WHAT HE DESIRES; TO CREATE FEAR AND CHAOS AND THUS DESTROY THE KINGDOM OF HEAVEN FOREVER!!
WHAT CAN WE DO?!
FOLLOW ME. I WILL KEEP YOU SAFE DURING EVEN THE MOST FIERY APOCALYPSE. WE SHALL RECLAIM OUR KINGDOM TOGETHER.

"BUT YOU MUST FIND MORE SOULS! THEY WILL ALL NEED OUR PROTECTION!"

"WE WILL, REVEREND! WE WILL!"

... I'M OUT.

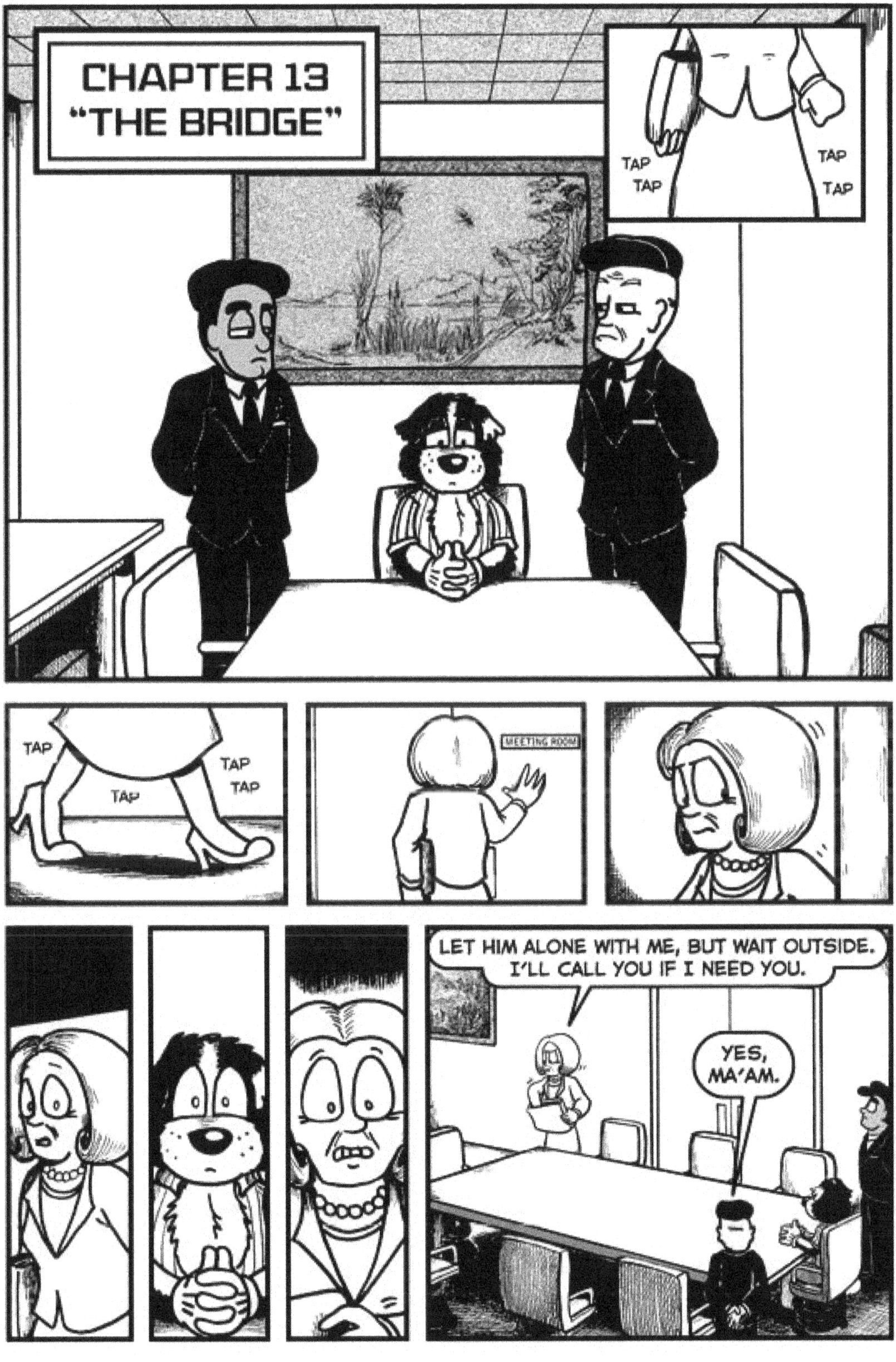

TAP
TAP
TAP
TAP

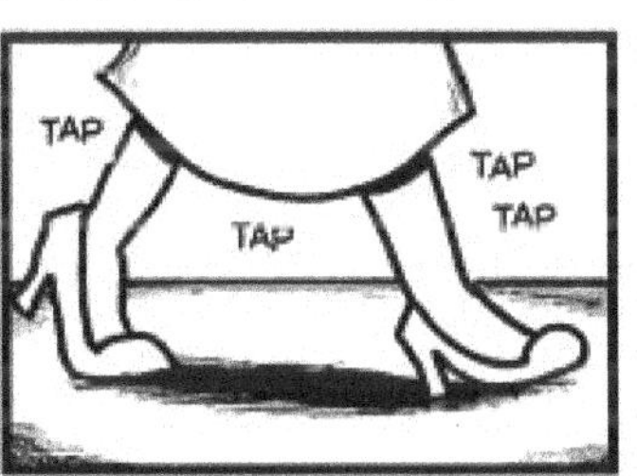
TAP
TAP
TAP
TAP

MEETING ROOM

LET HIM ALONE WITH ME, BUT WAIT OUTSIDE.
I'LL CALL YOU IF I NEED YOU.
YES, MA'AM.

"... I DON'T UNDERSTAND."

...YOU REALLY ARE JUST A DOG.

THAT'S RIGHT, MS. LA SALLE... JUST A DOG.
YOU EVEN TRIED AGAIN LAST NIGHT... BUT I FOUGHT YOU.

AND NOW I HAVE A POUNDING HEADACHE AND A BRAIN FOG THE SIZE OF SAN FRANCISCO.
THIS ISN'T RIGHT. THIS IS JUST NOT RIGHT.

HOW ARE YOU DOING THIS?!
MS. LA SALLE, I JUST WANT TO HELP.

THAT'S NOT ANSWERING MY QUESTION!!
"PLEASE LISTEN ... NELLIE WASN'T HELPING YOU. SHE DIDN'T SHARE YOUR INTERESTS."

SHE WAS ONLY TAKING YOUR MONEY SO SHE COULD DO HER OWN PROJECT.
YOU KNOW I'LL HAVE TO TAKE YOUR WORD FOR IT...

BECAUSE NONE OF THIS TELLS ME ANYTHING!!
YOU'RE LOOKING AT ME ALL WRONG.

IF IT WEREN'T FOR ME, YOU WOULDN'T HAVE THE CLARITY OF VISION TO ACHIEVE YOUR GOALS.

INSTEAD OF HAVING A CLEAR GRIFTER LIKE NELLIE FAKING HER "RESEARCH," YOU HAVE ME GIVING YOU EVERYTHING YOU NEED DIRECTLY.
"DIRECTLY?!"

LISTEN, POOCH, THE ONLY THING YOU'VE BEEN GIVING ME "DIRECTLY" IS YOUR MIND-ALTERING BULLSHIT!
THAT IS NOT SO.

I WANT MY OWN MIND BACK, DO YOU HEAR ME?! IF YOU'RE GOING TO HELP ME, YOU CAN HELP ME RIGHT NOW...

"...OR I CAN SEND YOU TO THE POUND."

... DO YOU FEEL LIKE YOU'LL LAST LONG ENOUGH TO SEND ME TO THE POUND?

EVERYTHING ALL RIGHT, MA'AM?
REINSTATE HIS BADGE. NOW.

HELLO, ARTHUR. GOOD MORNING, EVERYBODY.
MORNING, MS. HAYES!

WHERE'S EVA?
SHE'S...OUT.
THANK YOU, GISELE.

I'LL TAKE THIS TO THE OFFICE IF THAT'S OKAY. BIG DEADLINE TODAY, NEED AN EARLY START.
SURE, SHELLEY.

"ARTHUR, YOU COME VISIT ME LATER IF YOU WANT TO NAP ON THE OTTOMAN AGAIN."
"YES, MA'AM. THANK YOU!"

"HELLO!"

I'M HAPPY TO FINALLY MEET YOU. THAT WAS QUITE A SHOW YOU PUT ON!
...

...DON'T GET MIXED UP WITH THE REVEREND!
RELAX! I WON'T!

... WAIT. I'VE SEEN YOU SOMEPLACE BEFORE.
SIGH IT'LL COME TO YOU.
IN THE MEANTIME, I DON'T KNOW IF THIS'LL HELP YOU AS MUCH AS IT DID GARRETT, BUT...

GARRETT... GARRETT HILLMAN?
WAS HE HERE?!
YES.
I CAN ONLY ASSUME IT WAS BECAUSE OF YOUR INFLUENCE.

NO... NOT MY INFLUENCE... PROBABLY EAMONN'S.
WHO'S EAMONN?

NO, NO. I GO FIRST. WHO ARE YOU?
OH, VERY WELL. MY NAME IS HIKARU. I WAS VERNON SASAHARA'S DOG.

WELL, IT'S NICE TO--

...WAIT A MINUTE.

VERNON SASAHARA... FROM "SCIENCE ROX?"
YES.

THAT'S WHERE I'VE SEEN YOU! YOU PLAYED HIS DOG ON THAT SHOW!
I DIDN'T JUST PLAY HIM, I WAS HIS DOG.

YOU WERE THE ONE WHO SOFT-SHOED AND CHARLESTONED IN FRONT OF ARTIST RENDERINGS OF SINGULARITIES AND INTERFEROMETERS!
YES.

AND... OH YEAH! THOSE MELIES-STYLE EFFECTS WERE PART OF THE SHOW! YOU'D WAVE WHILE RIDING A "COMET" AS THE CREDITS ROLLED--
YES!!!
THANK YOU! IDENTITY CONFIRMED! PLEASE STOP!
... SORRY.
WE WEREN'T ON THE BEST OF TERMS WHEN HE PASSED AWAY.

I'M SORRY. IT'S, UM... NICE TO MEET YOU? FOR WHAT IT'S WORTH, I *LOVED* THE SHOW.
LET'S CHANGE THE SUBJECT. HOW HAVE YOU SURVIVED BEING GARRETT'S DOG?

WHAT? NO! I WAS *MIRANDA HAYES'* DOG! GARRETT WAS JUST HER ASSISTANT UNTIL HE TRIED TO SELL ME AND EAMONN.
OH MY.

IT'S A LONG STORY. WHY ARE YOU SO INTERESTED IN ME?
I'VE BEEN FOLLOWING YOU. I KNOW YOU'RE AT LEAST SOMEWHAT RESPONSIBLE FOR THE CHAOS AROUND HERE.
I CAN TELL YOU'RE AN ANIMAL OF DEEP PERCEPTION, SO LET US GET TO THE POINT.

I'M SURE, IN ALL YOUR WANDERINGS, YOU'VE FOUND OUT ABOUT THE HOLOGRAM PRINCIPLE.
... YES, I HAVE.

"AND?"
IT SOUNDED VERY CLOSE, BUT IT NEVER QUITE FIT IN TO WHAT I WAS EXPERIENCING.

... TO THE POINT WHERE YOU DON'T EVEN USE IT AS A STARTING REFERENCE WHEN EXPLAINING IT.
WELL, I MEAN, WHY CONFUSE THINGS FURTHER? IT'S CONFUSING ENOUGH AS IT IS.

EXACTLY. THE CURRENT SCIENTIFIC WORLD HAS SO MANY MODELS THAT DON'T ENTIRELY FIT WHAT'S HAPPENING TO US, AND TRYING TO MAKE THEM FIT IS PROBLEMATIC.
VERNON WANTED SO BADLY FOR MY EXPERIENCE TO JUSTIFY HIS TWIST ON STRING THEORY AND BLACK HOLE ENTROPY THAT HE NEVER REALLY LISTENED TO ME.

I MEAN, WE ARE JUST ANIMALS.
ANYTHING WE THINK IS INVALIDATED BY WHAT HUMANS DECIDE UPON ONCE THEY'VE OBSERVED US.

I SWEAR YOU SAID SOMETHING EARLIER ABOUT A "POINT" WE WERE GETTING TO.
EVA, DON'T MAKE THE MISTAKE I MADE.

DON'T LOOK TO HUMANS TO VERIFY WHAT'S GOING ON. IT IS IMPOSSIBLE. YOU WILL ALWAYS BE MISUNDERSTOOD. THIS IS ONLY FOR US TO COMPREHEND.
"WELL, I DON'T THINK THAT—"
YOU MUST TRUST ME.

VERNON WAS A SHOWBOATER, BUT HE WAS ALSO BRILLIANT. AND HE NEVER GOT IT.
LOOK, I APPRECIATE THE WARNING, BUT THIS IS VEERING CLOSE TO CANINE SUPREMACY RHETORIC, AND I'M NOT HERE FOR THAT.

THAT IS NOT WHAT I WAS TRYING TO —
WASN'T IT?

LISTEN TO ME. I JUST WANT TO LEARN, ALL RIGHT?

AND I'LL LEARN FROM WHOEVER I PLEASE!
EVA!!

COME ON, I'M NOWHERE NEAR READY TO TALK ABOUT LAST NIGHT...
EVA ...

THAT FIRST VOICE WAS ANOTHER ONE OF THOSE "ALIENS." EAMONN THINKS IT WAS WORKING FOR THE REVEREND.

I TOLD YOU HE WAS PERSUASIVE.
IT WAS TRAPPED.

...LIKE BOGS HAD BEEN.
OH, I SEE.

...THAT'S WHY YOU DECIDED TO SHOW US ANOTHER TALENT WE DIDN'T KNOW YOU HAD.
...

"NEVER AGAIN," HUH?
WE WILL COME BACK TO THIS, EAMONN. MARK MY WORDS.

RIGHT NOW, IT IS VERY CONCERNING THAT THE REVEREND HAS HIS OWN PRISONER AND A HUGE GROUP OF FOLLOWERS, ANY OF WHOM COULD START BRINGING HUMANS INTO THE PROJECTION EDGE...
... TO CONVERT.

YOUR "OTHER" IS USELESS. YOU MIGHT AS WELL LET IT GO.
WE WILL NOT DISARM IN THE FACE OF THIS THREAT.

IT WAS BAD TIMING, BUDDY. THE THING CAN DO IT RIGHT IF IT WANTS TO.
NO.

NOW THE REVEREND'S CORE FLOCK IS EVEN MORE ADHERED TO THEIR LEADER. THEIR CHURCH IS ALL BUT FIXED OVER THERE. I CAN'T MAKE IT GO AWAY.
NONE OF US CAN.

SUCH DEFEATISM.
"ANOTHER THING ..."

... I HAD TO "THREATEN" PRUDENCE.

SHE WAS FIGHTING ME IN HER SLEEP, AND THEN DURING THE DAY SHE CONFRONTED ME HEAD-ON. I HAD NO OTHER CHOICE.
WHAT DID YOU SAY?

"I IMPLIED THAT WITHOUT MY INFLUENCE, SHE WOULD DIE."

WHAT HAPPENED?!
HOW DID WE GET TO THIS POINT?!

WE USED TO BE ABLE TO QUIETLY DETER ANY ANIMAL WE COULD FIND, SO THAT THIS MENACING OTHERWORLD WOULD REMAIN UNDISCOVERED!
NOW WE'RE CONSCRIPTING "OTHERS" TO FIGHT DEMAGOGUES AND BLACK-MAILING CAPTAINS OF INDUSTRY...
IT'S INSANE!

THE CURE IS WORSE THAN THE ILLNESS!!
HORSEFEATHERS.

HUMANS DEAL WITH WARS ON A REGULAR BASIS, BUT ONCE THE WAR IS WON, THERE IS A PERIOD OF PEACE WHERE THE RAVAGES OF WAR ARE FORGOTTEN. THIS SHALL BE THE SAME.
SHE'S RIGHT.

"WE JUST MAY HAVE TO ASSIST HEAVILY WITH THE 'FORGETTING.'"

!

IS THAT EVEN *YOUR* CAR?
NOT NOW, FLUFFYPANTS. WE HAVE AN ENEMY IN THE KINGDOM OF HEAVEN.

MMM-HMM.
I DIDN'T TELL YOU THIS, FLUFFYPANTS...
BUT WHEN I FIRST ARRIVED AT THE KINGDOM OF HEAVEN, I HEARD A VOICE.

THAT VOICE CAME BACK. IT SEEMS THIS ENEMY IS *QUITE POWERFUL.*
WE LOST TOO MANY CHOSEN SOULS LAST NIGHT BECAUSE OF IT.
I NEED TO REGROUP MY THOUGHTS AND FIND A WAY TO *FIGHT* THIS ENEMY.

OH YES. I KNOW YOU'VE LOST AT LEAST *ONE* OF YOUR "CHOSEN SOULS."
WHAT? WHO?

"EUGENE."   "WHICH ONE WAS HE?"
WHY COULDN'T I HAVE GRABBED SOME MORE *FOOD* BEFORE I LEFT?!

I DON'T KNOW HOW IT HAPPENS, EVA! IT JUST FEELS LIKE SOMETHING I CAN'T HELP DOING WHEN THINGS GET... BAD.
I WANT IT TO STOP. I WANT IT NOT TO HAPPEN. I'VE TRIED TO SUPPRESS IT BUT IT SEEMS I NEVER SUCCEED!!
I DON'T WANT TO CAUSE ANY MORE SUFFERING!
FOR THE LAST TIME, LET'S NOT GET AHEAD OF THINGS.
WE HAVE NO REAL IDEA IF YOU EVEN PLAYED A PART IN WHAT HAPPENED TO DONNELLY OR NELLIE. WE NEED TO LEARN MORE ABOUT WHAT'S HAPPENING TO YOU.
"I'VE MET SOMEONE WHO HAS MORE EXPERIENCE WITH ALL THIS THAN ME."
"BUT HOW CAN WE DO THAT?"
YOU MEAN, AT THE PROJECTION EDGE? WHEN? WHO?
"THIS MORNING, AND YOU'LL SEE. HE MIGHT HAVE SOME INSIGHT INTO YOUR SITUATION. HE'S OUR BEST HOPE, AT ANY RATE."
SIGH ... RIGHT, SO.

... OH, IT'S YOU.

I WAS WORRIED FOR A MOMENT THAT GARRETT MIGHT HAVE FOUND ME AGAIN. RELAX. I'M WAITING FOR SOMEONE ELSE.

IS THIS... PART OF THE "KINGDOM OF HEAVEN"?
THAT MEANS A DIFFERENT THING IN JAPANESE MYTHOLOGY.

THAT'S WHAT THE REVEREND SAID THIS WAS. THOUGH IT NEVER LOOKED LIKE THIS.
I'M AFRAID THE FELLOW DOESN'T KNOW WHAT HE'S TALKING ABOUT. BUT I THINK YOU KNEW THAT.

YES... I DID, ACTUALLY.

BUT I'D HOPED I WOULDN'T COME BACK HERE AFTER I LEFT THE CHOSEN SOULS. YET HERE I AM. AM I GOING TO BE COMING HERE EVERY TIME I GO TO SLEEP?
PERHAPS. IT'S POSSIBLE TO AVOID IT BUT IT TAKES TREMENDOUS WILLPOWER.

IT WON'T MATTER, HOWEVER. SOON THIS WILL AFFECT US ALL DURING THE DAYTIME AS WELL.

THE CHAOS IS GROWING AS THE GAME BECOMES TOP-HEAVY WITH PLAYERS, ALL OUT TO WIN.

... EVEN IF SOME OF THE PLAYERS THINK THEY CAN WIN BY TYING ONE HAND BEHIND THEIR BACKS.

HELLO, HIKARU. ER... SORRY FOR MY MELTDOWN THE LAST TIME WE MET.
IT'S UNDERSTANDABLE. WE ARE FACED WITH A LOT.

I'M, UM, REALLY IMPRESSED WITH WHAT YOU'VE CREATED HERE. THE DRAGON IS A NICE TOUCH.
SHE WASN'T EVEN INTENDED, BUT SHE FITS IN NICELY.

...YOU DON'T SAY.
I'M SORRY, HAVE YOU MET... EUGENE, ISN'T IT?
WELL, YES... BUT I DON'T REMEMBER MENTIONING...

I'LL EXPLAIN LATER. YOU DO LOOK FAMILIAR.
I USED TO BE ONE OF THE REVEREND'S "CHOSEN SOULS." I WAS THERE LAST NIGHT WHEN YOU INTERRUPTED HIS SERMON.

OH.
I'VE LEFT THEM NOW. I DON'T KNOW WHAT ALL THAT STUFF WAS, WHETHER YOU OR THE REVEREND CAUSED IT, BUT I'VE HAD ENOUGH. BUT NOW... UM...

...HIKARU. SHE JUST SAID IT.
... HIKARU HERE SAYS I MIGHT BE HERE EVERY NIGHT WHEN I'M ASLEEP. I CAN'T STAND THAT! I'LL GO CRAZY!!

EUGENE, IT DOESN'T HAVE TO BE LIKE THIS.
I DON'T CARE! IT'S STILL TOO CRAZY! I WANT TO HAVE A NORMAL LIFE AGAIN!
"EUGENE..."

... COME WITH US. WE'LL SHOW YOU WHAT THIS CAN REALLY BE. I'M TOTES SURE YOU'LL FEEL BETTER!

"MORE FRIENDS OF YOURS?"
"YES...WHICH REMINDS ME..."

THIS IS EAMONN, WHOM I'VE MENTIONED BEFORE.
I SEE.

!

WHAT THE DEVIL ARE YOU DOING?!
TELL ME. HAVE YOU HAD EPISODES WHERE YOU WEREN'T ABLE TO CONTROL YOURSELF? WHERE YOUR VIOLENT EMOTIONS TRANSLATED INTO PANDEMONIUM?

AH ... DEFINE "PANDEMONIUM."
I THINK YOU KNOW WHAT I MEAN. YOUR EMOTIONS CAUSE YOU TO MANIFEST YOURSELF IN MIND-WARPING WAYS.

HOW DO YOU KNOW ABOUT THIS?
I'VE WITNESSED IT BEFORE. AND TO BE HONEST, I DON'T WISH TO WITNESS IT AGAIN.

YOU HAVE NO ADVICE ON HOW TO CONTROL IT?
NONE. APART FROM WHAT YOU SEE HERE, MY OWN ABILITIES AROUND HERE ARE LIMITED.

I WAS NEVER ABLE TO MAKE THE PROJECTION EDGE WORK "FOR" ME IN A MEANINGFUL WAY.
ONCE VERNON PASSED AWAY, I DECIDED THIS PLANE WAS TOO MUCH FOR ME. I WANTED NO PART OF IT. SO I FORCED MYSELF TO STAY AWAY.

WHAT CHANGED YOUR MIND?
MY MIND WAS CHANGED FOR ME. AND BESIDES, I'M BORED. I NOW WANT EVERY PART OF IT.
失礼します。

楽しかったが、パーティーは終わったよう。

I FEEL SO MUCH BETTER NOW... SO CALM...
IT DOESN'T ALWAYS HAVE TO BE SO BAD.

I DON'T KNOW WHEN I'VE EVER KNOWN LIFE TO BE GOOD. I MEAN, DEALING WITH KINGMAKER WAS WEIRD, BUT IT WAS WORTH IT JUST TO FINALLY GET A SOFT BED AND REGULAR MEALS.

BUT WHEN THE REVEREND GOT INVOLVED... THINGS JUST CHANGED.
I KNOW HOW YOU FEEL.

BUT THIS EXPERIENCE DOESN'T HAVE TO BE DEFINED BY THE REVEREND.
IT CAN HELP YOU.
I SEE WHAT YOU MEAN ... IT'S SO—

CRACK

WHAT'S HAPPENING NOW?! WHAT DID SHE SAY?!
SHE SAID, "THE PARTY'S OVER."
WHAT DOES THAT MEAN?!
I WOULD RATHER NOT FIND OUT! WE MUST GET OFF THIS BRIDGE!
RUMBLE RUMBLE
RUMBLE RUMBLE
RUMBLE RUMBLE RUMBLE
RUMBLE RUMBLE RUMBLE RUMBLE
RUMBLE RUMBLE
CRASH
CRACK
BOOM
IT'S TOO LATE!!
RUMBLE RUMBLE
CRASH
CRACK
ROAR
RUMBLE RUMBLE RUMBLE
RUMBLE RUMBLE RUMBLE
RUMBLE RUMBLE
RUMBLE RUMBLE
THWOOM
WHAT'S HAPPENING UNDERNEATH US?!
... I HAVE NO IDEA.
... BUT WE'LL ALL HAVE AN IDEA IN A SECOND.
KRICK
RUMBLE RUMBLE RUMBLE RUMBLE RUMBLE RUMBLE RUMBLE RUMBLE

CRACK!
RUMBLE RUMBLE RUMBLE RUMBLE
RUMBLE RUMBLE RUMBLE RUMBLE RUMBLE
RUMBLE
RUMBLE
CRASH

CHAPTER 14
"UNCOMMON GROUND"

I'LL NEVER GET TO SLEEP. DAMMIT, WHY DOES MY HEAD HURT SO MUCH? IS THIS THING GIVING ME BRAIN CANCER NOW?!

SINCE I STARTED INVESTIGATING THAT VOICE IT'S BEEN LIKE THIS CONSTANTLY. I SWEAR, IF THIS IS ITS ATTEMPT TO DETER ME, I'LL KILL IT BEFORE IT KILLS ME.

SPLOOSH!
SPLURSH!
SPLASH!

... THIS ISN'T PART OF YOUR ORIGINAL DIORAMA, IS IT?
I DON'T KNOW WHERE WE ARE.

THIS FEELS REAL TO ME, EVA! WHAT IS IT?
IT DOES FEEL MORE TACTILE...

THE AIR IS NOXIOUS... THE WATER IS STICKY... AND WHAT EXACTLY ARE WE ON?!
THIS RAIN SMELLS LIKE WEE!!

...AMMONIA RAIN. THERE'S SOMETHING I CAN CROSS OFF MY BUCKET LIST.
EVA, HOW DID WE EVEN--

HELP!

... MY APOLOGIES. I APPARENTLY... FELL OFF.
FELL OFF? FELL OFF OF WHAT?!

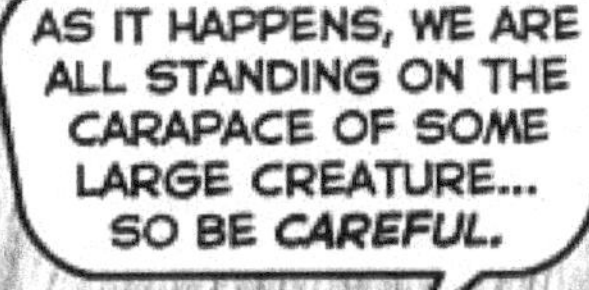

AS IT HAPPENS, WE ARE ALL STANDING ON THE CARAPACE OF SOME LARGE CREATURE... SO BE CAREFUL.

HELLO!! IS THERE SOMEONE DOWN THERE?!

HELLO EAMONN.

BOGS!!

IS THIS WHERE YOU LIVE? IS THIS YOUR REAL EXISTENCE?!
I AM NOT BEING SOCIAL.

...I SUPPOSE NOT. IF YOU WERE BEING SOCIAL, YOU WOULD'VE POLITELY INVITED US AND NOT HAD YOUR FAKE DRAGON FRIEND CAUSE US TO PLUMMET HERE.
EVA! DON'T ANTAGONIZE HIM!

I DON'T FEEL AS IF WE CAN WAKE UP FROM THIS!
WE HAVE FOUND THERE IS ANOTHER OF OUR KIND BEING HELD PRISONER.

... OH BOY.

STALLING WOULD NOT BE A GOOD IDEA.
HONEST...UM..."BOGS"... WE FOUND OUT ABOUT THIS OURSELVES JUST THIS MORNING!!

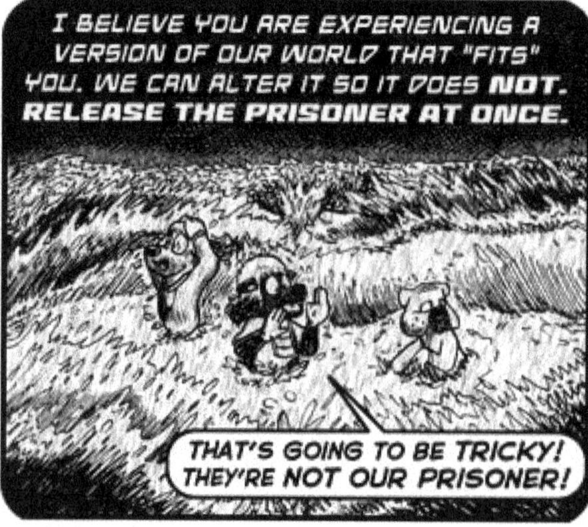

I BELIEVE YOU ARE EXPERIENCING A VERSION OF OUR WORLD THAT "FITS" YOU. WE CAN ALTER IT SO IT DOES NOT. RELEASE THE PRISONER AT ONCE.
THAT'S GOING TO BE TRICKY! THEY'RE NOT OUR PRISONER!

I FEEL AS IF MY HEAD IS FILLED WITH EVERY BOOK IN THE WORLD ... AND THEY'RE ALL TRANSLATED INTO PIG GIBBERISH.

COUGH
GASP

EVA... I CAN'T WAKE MYSELF UP...
YOU'RE DOING A DAMN GOOD JOB OF KEEPING US PRISONER RIGHT NOW!!
YOU ARE BECOMING A THREAT TO US.

LOOK! EAMONN WANTS TO MAKE UP FOR WHAT HE ACCIDENTALLY DID TO YOU. WE ALL DO! WHY DON'T YOU AT LEAST LET US LOOK INTO THIS? WE MIGHT BE ABLE TO FREE YOUR FRIEND!

WE DO NOT TRUST YOU.
NONE OF US WANT TO SEE ANYONE SUFFER!
EAMONN SURE DOESN'T!
LET US GO!
GIVE US A CHANCE TO FIND OUT WHAT'S GOING ON!!

WE WILL GIVE YOU A SHORT TIME.

... HOW SHORT?

... AT LAST.

WHAT HAPPENED?
CLICK

STILL CAN'T HELP THIS FEELING ...
LIKE THERE'S SOMETHING ABOUT TO BURST OPEN INSIDE ME...

I JUST SAW THAT DOG AGAIN.
YES, HE'S HERE FOR GOOD. I'VE ADOPTED HIM.

"YOU'VE WHAT??!"
I HAVE ADOPTED HIM. HE HAS NO HOME, SO HE'S STAYING HERE.

PRUDENCE, YOU DON'T EVEN LIKE DOGS!
THIS ONE'S... SPECIAL.

LOOKS LIKE JUST ANOTHER SCROUNGY BATHMAT TO ME.
CAN YOU DO ME A FAVOR AND NOT QUESTION ME ABOUT THIS? JUST GIVE HIM A WIDE BERTH AND HE'LL LEAVE YOU ALONE, ALL RIGHT?!

MARCEL!
WE HAVE AN INTERESTING CASE FOR YOU.
HIS NAME IS HORACE... ANOTHER MIXED BREED. HIS OWNER SAYS HE'S HAD SOME SORT OF TRAUMATIC EXPERIENCE AND HIS WHOLE MOOD HAS BECOME WITHDRAWN.
Chehalis PET CARE

WHAT KIND OF EXPERIENCE?
HE WON'T OPEN UP ABOUT IT AT ALL. BUT THERE'S SOMETHING TELLING ME THAT YOUR BACKGROUND IN CANINE MENTAL HEALTH WILL BE VERY USEFUL.

"HORACE?"
CLICK CLICK CLICK

... I'D LIKE YOU TO MEET MARCEL.

CLICK CLICK CLICK

WHAT DID THEY MEAN BY "A SHORT TIME?"
WHO KNOWS HOW THEY MEASURE TIME? IT DOESN'T MATTER. URGENCY SHOULD BE A FACTOR HERE.

DOES THIS MEAN CONFRONTING THE REVEREND AGAIN?
YES. BUT I THINK HE'S "WOUNDED" THIS TIME, SO IT MIGHT BE EASIER THAN THE LAST TIME.

AND, UH... DO WE EVEN KNOW HOW TO "FREE" AN ALIEN?
"NO. WE'LL HAVE TO LEARN ON THE JOB."

I'M IN. I CAN'T KEEP RUNNING AWAY.
ME TOO, DEFO.
DO YOU THINK THAT HIKARU LAD WILL HELP US?

HE'S THE ONE WHO SOUGHT ME OUT ORIGINALLY, PLUS HE SAID HE WANTED "EVERY PART" OF THIS. I DON'T SEE WHY HE WOULDN'T HELP.

SO THERE. I AM RESOLVED.
I AM STAYING AS FAR AWAY FROM THE PROJECTION EDGE AS I CAN UNTIL I UNDERSTAND WHAT JUST HAPPENED LAST NIGHT.

...I'M SORRY, I THINK WE ALREADY HAVE A RELIGION.
WE'RE LOOKING FOR A DOG WHO CALLS HIM- SELF "THE REVEREND."

I'M AFRAID HE'S NOT HERE. DO YOU HAVE HIS PHONE NUMBER?
HE DOESN'T ANSWER HIS PHONE.
...LAND SAKES.

WOULD YOU TELL HIM THAT HÅKON JØRGENSEN, ATTORNEY FOR GIDEON BEST'S ESTATE, WAS HERE.
HIS HEIRS HAVE DRAWN UP PLANS FOR THIS MANSION AND THEY WON'T BE NEEDING THE REVEREND'S SERVICES IN FOUR WEEKS.

PLEASE LET HIM KNOW TIME IS OF THE ESSENCE.

... I'LL TELL HIM.

I THINK BUDDY'S RIGHT, GRÄUBEN. WE SHOULD SWITCH TO THE EAMONN PROBLEM.
VERY WELL. SHOULD WE CONFRONT HIM DIRECTLY?

... YOU'VE SEEN WHAT HAPPENS.
YES, MONSTERS, CHAOS, MADNESS, AND GENERAL UNPLEASANTNESS.

BUT SURELY, BUDDY, YOU COULD TRY. YOU'VE ALWAYS TAKEN PRIDE IN YOUR REASONABLE, AFFABLE NATURE.

I'M NOT SURE EVEN THE DALAI LAMA COULD SELL "YOU'VE GOT TO KILL YOURSELF FOR THE GOOD OF THE UNIVERSE."
!!

GOOD LORD, MAN, DID YOU ACTUALLY THINK WE'D NEED TO GO THAT FAR?!
THE REALITY IS THAT'S WHAT IT'LL TAKE TO GET HIM TO STOP.
"NOT NECESSARILY."

WE JUST NEED TO ISOLATE HIM FROM HIS FRIENDS. WE NEED TO BE A LARGER REAL-LIFE INFLUENCE THAN THEY ARE.

YOU MEAN... ABDUCT HIM. LIKE THE LAST TIME WE DISCOVERED A TROUBLEMAKER.
THAT'S RIGHT.

ISOLATE HIM IN BOTH WORLDS, SO WE CAN HELP HIM SEE REASON WITHOUT DISTRACTIONS.
EAMONN'S DIFFERENT FROM THAT ANEMIC BIEWER TERRIER WE FOUND TWO YEARS AGO.

HIS FIRE IS MUCH, MUCH STRONGER.
I THINK IT'S A GOOD PLAN.

TWO OF THE "ILLUMINATI CHASERS" LIVE IN IDAHO, SO IT'S PERFECT.
!!!

WAIT — WE'RE NOT GOING TO USE THAT RIDICULOUS "SECRET SOCIETY" YOUR OWNER BELONGS TO AGAIN, ARE WE?!
"OF COURSE."

TITUS. THEY ARE MORONS.
THEY ARE PLIABLE. THAT'S ALL THAT MATTERS.

ALL RIGHT. ON ONE CONDITION.
YOU LET ME TRY THIS MY WAY FIRST.

WE HAD BETTER HAVE MORE LUCK TONIGHT.

TWO NIGHTS WE'VE HAD LISTENING TO THE REVEREND'S MONEYGRUBBING AND THERE'S BEEN NO HINT OF AN ALIEN OR HOW TO FREE HIM.

IF WE DON'T SENSE THE ALIEN'S PRESENCE TONIGHT, THAT'S IT FOR DISCRETION. WE'LL HAVE TO CONFRONT THE REVEREND DIRECTLY ONCE AND FOR ALL. LET'S GO.

UM... GUYS?

"HELLO, BIJOU!"

HOW'D YOU LIKE TO GO FOR A RIDE?

B

YOU GUYS GO ON.

I TOTES GOT THIS.

WELL, ARTHUR, I THINK IT'S TIME YOU JOINED YOUR FRIENDS AND WENT TO BED.
AWWW ...

COULDN'T YOU READ TO ME AGAIN TONIGHT? I COULD EASILY FALL ASLEEP RIGHT HERE!
WELL ...

I WANT TO HEAR MORE ABOUT THE TIGER PRINCE!
OH ... WELL, I AM FLATTERED YOU LIKE THAT.

"PLEASE?"
ALL RIGHT. YOU'RE GETTING A BIT UNDER MY SKIN, BUT IT'S NICE TO KNOW SOMEONE LIKES THIS.
TALES OF THE
TIGER PRINCE
by Shelley Hayes

SUCH IRONY. ANDERSON MCNEAL THOUGHT THIS BOOK WAS A FAILURE AND NOW I'VE APPARENTLY FOUND THE AUDIENCE OF ONE IT APPEALS TO.
OKAY... "'THE TIGER PRINCE AND THE MERCHANT COATIMUNDI.' THE PRINCE'S SERVANTS AWOKE. WHEN THEY CHECKED THEIR MASTER'S ROYAL BEJEWELED SUITE, THEY DISCOVERED HE WAS NOT IN HIS BED! NOR WAS HE IN HIS BATHROOM! SUCH A MYSTERY!"

IT'S GOOD TO SEE YOU AGAIN, BIJOU...
HOW COME YOU DIDN'T TELL ME?

... BECAUSE IT WASN'T A GOOD IDEA.
WHAT DO YOU MEAN? YOU MUST'VE DONE ALL SORTS OF THINGS! MAYBE WE COULD HAVE SAVED GIDEON BEST!

AND THEN... WHAT YOU DID TO ADAM! HOW COULD YOU DO THAT? I THOUGHT YOU WERE MY FRIEND!
I AM YOUR FRIEND.

... DESPITE WHAT I'M DOING NOW.. THIS... ALL THIS... IS NOT A GAME.
I KNOW!

DO YOU?
THAT WAS WHERE I WENT WRONG. WHEN I LET YOU GO ON ABOUT YOUR FRIENDS, I FELT I SHOULD LET YOU HAVE YOUR FUN.
GOD KNEW NELLIE WOULD NEVER STOP, NO MATTER WHAT I DID, AND SINCE YOU WERE HAVING A GOOD TIME, WHO WAS I TO INTERFERE?

"NO MATTER WHAT I DID?!!"
... BUT THAT WAS BEFORE I FOUND OUT WHO ONE OF YOUR FRIENDS REALLY WAS.

"NO MATTER WHAT I DID??!!"
I WAS ONLY TRYING TO SUBTLY DISCOURAGE HER. BUT EVEN DOING THAT HAD DANGEROUS CONSEQUENCES.

THAT'S WHAT I'M TRYING TO TELL YOU, BIJOU! THIS PLACE ISN'T SAFE! EVERY ANIMAL SHOULD STAY AWAY FROM IT!
BUT YOU'RE GOOD TO CREATE THIS "KARTSCAPE" TO MAKE YOUR SILLY PUPPY FRIEND FEEL BETTER.

SOUNDS A LOT LIKE "THIS IS OKAY FOR THE RIGHT ANIMALS BUT NOT THE ONES I DON'T APPROVE OF."
NOT EVERYONE IS EQUIPPED TO TREAT THIS EXPERIENCE RESPONSIBLY; YOU KNOW THAT. ALL IT TAKES IS ONE BAD APPLE.
HELP ME

WOULD YOU WANT THE REVEREND TWISTING THIS TO HURT PEOPLE?
OH, YOU KNOW ABOUT THE REVEREND TOO. WHY AM I NOT SURPRISED.

... WE KNOW ABOUT A LOT OF THINGS.

"WE...?!"

I CAN'T SAFEGUARD THIS "ULTIMATE HORIZON" ALL BY MYSELF. THERE ARE OTHERS HELPING ME. WE'RE SORT OF A... PROTECTIVE SOCIETY. WE MAKE SURE NOTHING GOES WRONG.
... I CAN'T BELIEVE THIS.

YOU'VE HAD THIS DOUBLE LIFE ALL THIS TIME... AND YOU NEVER TOLD ME A THING. FRIENDS DON'T DO THIS! NICE PEOPLE DON'T DO THIS!
BIJOU, PLEASE UNDERSTAND.

I'VE KNOWN ABOUT THIS PLACE FOR A LONG TIME, AND I'VE LEARNED A LOT ABOUT HOW IT WORKS. AND NOW I NEED YOUR HELP.

"SEE, IT'S YOUR FRIEND, EAMONN. YOU MAY HAVE NOTICED HE HAS A KIND OF INFLUENCE HERE THAT HE CAN'T CONTROL."

"IF HE CONTINUES THE WAY HE HAS, HE COULD END UP HURTING OTHERS AND I KNOW YOU DON'T..."
HOLD IT.

WHAT'S THAT?
B

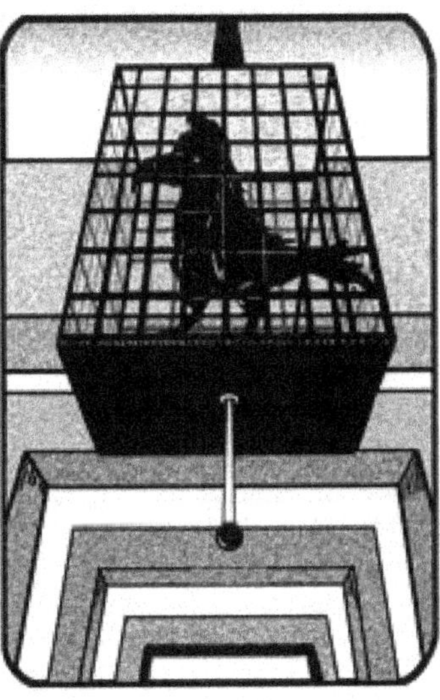

I DON'T REMEMBER ANY GIANT CAGED BLACKBIRDS IN THE GAMES WE PLAYED.
... NO.

THEN WHAT—

THE TRAPPED ALIEN ISN'T THE REVEREND'S PRISONER AT ALL — IT'S YOURS!
...

SIGH IT WAS... "THE SOCIETY'S" DECISION. I ONLY WENT ALONG WITH IT. THAT ISN'T AN ...
... EXCUSE ...

... NO. STOP. DON'T. COME BACK.

HELLO...
MY NAME IS BIJOU.

... ARE YOU ALL RIGHT?

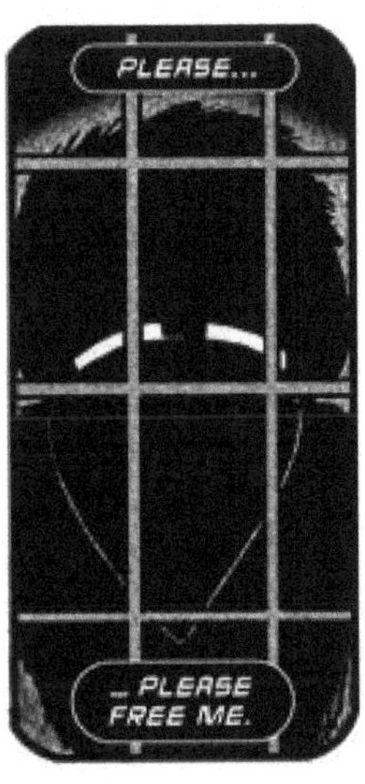

PLEASE...
... PLEASE FREE ME.

WHERE AM I GONNA GET THE KEY FOR THIS?

... I DON'T NEED A KEY.

RATTLE
CRUMBLE
RATTLE

RATTLE CRUMBLE
RATTLE
RATTLE
RATTLE RATTLE

B
O
O
M
B
L
A
M

151

"OH, BIJOU ... "

I REALLY MISJUDGED YOU...

I MEAN, YOU'RE STILL EVERY BIT AS KIND AND GENEROUS AS I ONCE BELIEVED ...

BUT NOW I KNOW YOU MUST BE STOPPED.

BIJOU! ARE YOU ALL RIGHT? WHAT HAPPENED?

IT'S ALL RIGHT ... THE ALIEN'S FREE. IT WAS BUDDY'S PRISONER, NOT THE REVEREND'S.
... OH.

... YEAH ...
I DON'T THINK BUDDY IS MY FRIEND ANYMORE.

NEW LIFE SHOWERS
LIFE SHOWE

SNIFF SNIFF
COLORADO STATE FAIR 2016
... HM.
SO THIS IS WHAT "CLEAN" SMELLS LIKE.

Canine Rehabilitation Center
LOOKS CLOSE...

UH, HI. IS THIS THE CANINE REHAB CENTER?
YES! COME ON IN!

YES, UM... I'M INTERESTED IN FINDING A JOB... DOING THE WHOLE REHAB THING...
WELL, THAT'S TERRIFIC! ARE YOU ABLE TO FILL OUT A FORM?

UH, NO, I CAN'T WRITE...
THAT'S FINE, I'LL HELP YOU. HAVE A SEAT.

"MAY I ASK WHAT BROUGHT YOU HERE?"
WELL... I'VE HAD A SORT OF WEIRD EXPERIENCE THAT KINDA CHANGED MY LIFE...

AND I FIGURED I'D BETTER STRAIGHTEN MYSELF OUT IN CASE I HAVE TO DEAL WITH IT AGAIN.

CLICK
CLICK
CLICK
CLICK CLICK

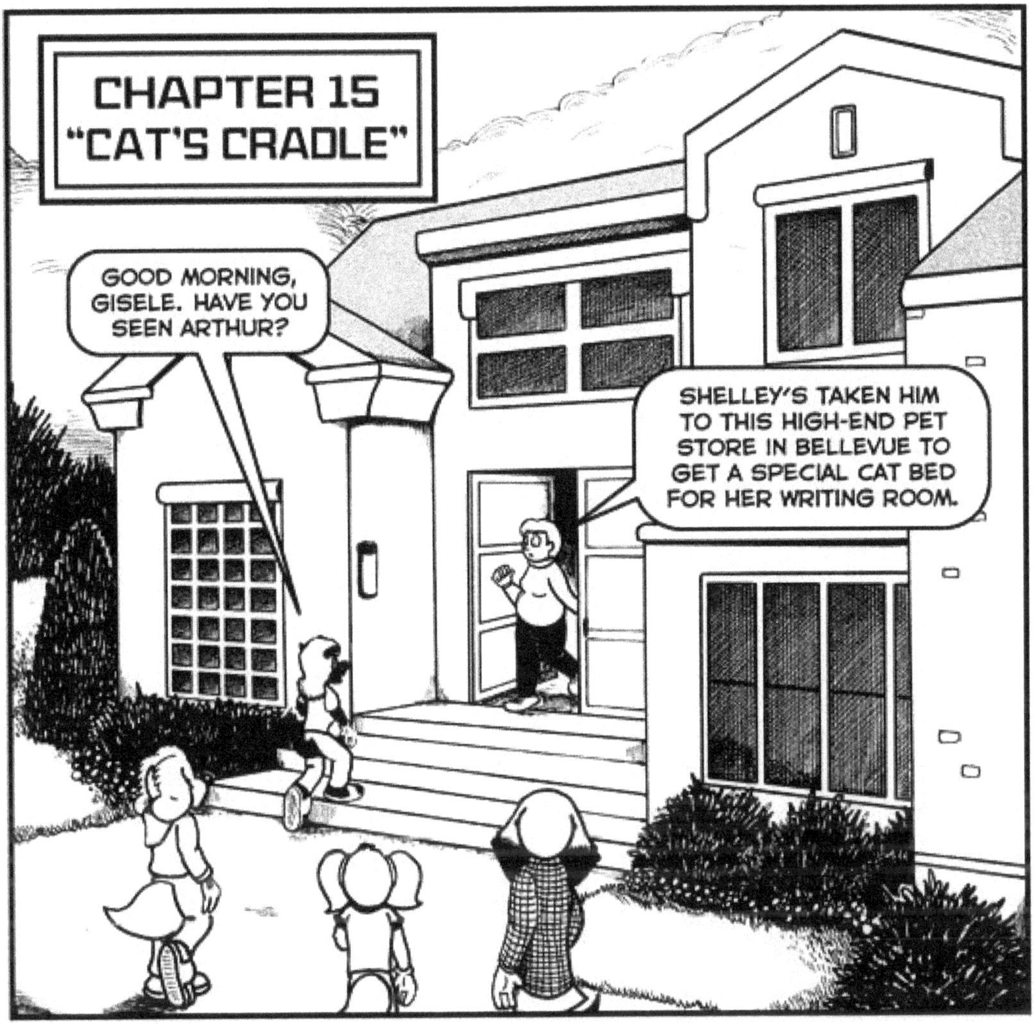

CHAPTER 15 "CAT'S CRADLE"

RIGHT NOW I'M JUST THANKFUL THAT WE'VE PLACATED OUR "FOREIGN FRIENDS." THEY'RE CLEARLY MORE DANGEROUS THAN THEY ORIGINALLY LET ON. WE'RE GOING TO HAVE TO BE CAREFUL.

THANK YOU, GISELE. IT LOOKS DELICIOUS.
YES, THANK YOU.

... YOU KNOW, IT'S A BIT WEIRD THAT WE HAVEN'T SEEN ANY CATS, WHEN YOU THINK ABOUT IT.
HMM. I'D ALWAYS ASSUMED CATS WERE JUST AS INTUITIVE, BUT YOU'RE RIGHT... NOT A ONE.

CATS CAN DO THIS. I HAD TWO OF THEM AS FRIENDS WHEN I WAS A PUPPY.
THEN WHY HAVEN'T WE SEEN ANY?

PAF
!

... HOW COULD YOU DO THAT.

I'M SORRY TITUS CAN'T PLAY GOLF ANYMORE, BUT WE DON'T NEED TO BE TORTURING INNOCENT LIFE FORMS.
"INNOCENT."
THESE ENABLING MONSTERS WHO TREAT THIS PLACE AS IF IT WERE DISNEYLAND.

THAT DOESN'T EXCUSE US LOCKING THEM AWAY.
WE ARE RETURNING TO OUR ORIGINAL PLAN REGARDING EAMONN. IS THAT CLEAR?

YES.
"I'LL LET TITUS KNOW HE CAN CONTACT HIS OWNER AND..."

WAIT.

LISTEN. IF WE JUST HAVE THEM RAID SHELLEY HAYES' HOUSE FOR EAMONN, THEY'LL LIKELY SCREW IT UP AND END UP IN JAIL.
YOU KNOW IT. I KNOW IT.

"I HAVE AN IDEA TO MAKE THIS GO MORE... SMOOTHLY. BUT I NEED YOUR HELP."

... GO ON.
YOU'RE A CAT.

... NOW THAT WE'VE VERIFIED THAT YOU'RE OBSERVANT, CONTINUE.
I NEED TO KNOW ABOUT YOUR ... INTRODUCTION TO THIS PLACE.

I TOLD YOU WE'D BE IN TROUBLE! IF BEST'S HEIRS DISCOVER WE'VE BEEN RUNNING A MUTT HOSTEL, WE'LL BE SHOT, GASSED AND THEN TAKEN TO COURT!
CAN'T EVEN HAVE A SMOKE... JUST MAKES IT WORSE...
A WHOLE DAMN WEEK WITH NO SMOKES...

ARE YOU EVEN LISTENING TO ME?!
YES! AND I WISH I WASN'T! BE QUIET!! I CAN'T EVEN...

OH MY GOD.

CLICK WHIRR

WHAT ARE YOU...
FOR FUCK'S SAKE, CAT, SHUT UP AND GO AWAY.
TAP CLICK TAP TAP

... YET I PERSEVERED.
HMM. DOES THAT HAPPEN TO ALL CATS OR WAS IT JUST YOU?

CATS' PSYCHES ARE HIGHLY INDIVIDUALISTIC.
AS SUCH, EVERY CAT'S EXPERIENCE WILL VARY. IT COULD BE PAINLESS AND SIMPLE... OR TORTUROUS AND CHAOTIC. NO ONE CAN TELL.
MAYBE WE SHOULDN'T DO THIS, THEN.

I DON'T WANT ARTHUR TO GET HURT. BUT HE'S OUR LAST EASY HOPE TO GET AT EAMONN.
ALL RIGHT, HERE IS WHAT I PROPOSE.

I WILL DO WHAT I CAN TO PUT HIS MIND AT EASE.

...YOU?!

FOR YOUR INFORMATION, I HAVE DISCOVERED THE PRESENCE OF ANOTHER FELINE GOES VERY FAR TOWARDS HELPING A CAT ADJUST TO THIS PLANE.
BETWEEN MY CALMING EFFECT AND YOUR STATUS AS PROTECTOR AND GUARDIAN, YOUR FRIEND WILL DECIDEDLY FEEL SAFE AND RELAXED.

...FINE.

BIJOU... I'M SORRY YOUR FRIEND TURNED OUT NOT TO BE WHO YOU THOUGHT HE WAS.
YOU KNOW...

I KINDA THOUGHT ABOUT IT. EVEN AT NEUROSMITH, I BARELY EVER LOOKED HIM IN THE EYE. AND I REALIZED WHY... IF I HAD, I WOULDA SEEN HE WAS LYING TO ME... AND I DIDN'T WANT TO KNOW.

I'M SURE HE DID IMAGINE IT WAS ALL FOR YOUR PROTECTION ...

... BUT ...

ER... EVERYTHING ALL RIGHT THERE, LADS?

... IT'S HIM. I KNOW IT IS.
... YEAH.

... WHAT DO YOU MEAN?!
HE'S THE ONE WHO'S SCREWED US ALL UP. WE CAN'T HUNT. WE CAN'T SMELL. WE CAN BARELY SLEEP, AND WE CAN'T EVEN THINK. WE'VE SEEN HIM. WE KNOW HE'S DOING THIS!!

I --
GET HIM!

DON'T TRY TO FIGHT THEM, BIJOU!! RUN!!

JUMP IN!
SPLASH!

YOU CAN'T STAY OUT THERE FOREVER! WE'LL WAIT ALL DAY!

PADDLE TO THE STEPS ON THE OTHER SIDE OF THE HOUSE! THEY CAN'T GET US THERE!

WHAT HAPPENED, EAMONN?! I'VE NEVER SEEN ANYTHING LIKE THAT! WERE THEY RABID?

I... DON'T KNOW.

"AT LENGTH, THE TIGER PRINCE ROSE AND WAVED HIS PAWS FOR SILENCE. 'FRIENDS, I WANT TO THANK YOU FOR THIS MAGNIFICENT FEAST.'"
CAT ON BOARD!

"'I AM HUMBLED BY YOUR FRIENDSHIP. IT IS AN HONOR TO SERVE AS YOUR PRINCE.' HIS RETINUE CHEERED AS ANOTHER BOLD ADVENTURE CAME TO A CLOSE WITH THE SETTING OF THE REGAL, ROSY SIR SUN."

I MAY WRITE A FEW MORE OF THOSE ...

TWITCH — TWITCH —

"ARTHUR."

BUDDY...?
HI, LI'L FELLA.

WHAT IS THIS ...
THIS IS WHAT BIJOU'S BEEN DOING AT NIGHT. AND NOW YOU'RE DOING IT TOO.

"WOW... IT FEELS SO WEIRD... SO WEIRD... I'M AFRAID... "
"NOW, DON'T BE AFRAID. I'M HERE. I BROUGHT YOU SAFE AND SOUND TO BIJOU AND EVA, DIDN'T I?"
THIS BOY HAS POOR JUDGMENT IN CHOOSING FICTIONAL HEROES...

"OH YES! AND SHELLEY HAYES! SHE'S WONDERFUL! SHE'S A GREAT WRITER, BUDDY!"
AH ...

"SHE WRITES ALL ABOUT AN AMAZING TIGER PRINCE WHO GOES ON ALL SORTS OF ADVENTURES! HE'S LIKE..."

"Now, now, lad..."
...
...

I am certainly much more than "amazing."

"ARE YOU...?"
YES, IT IS I, ARTHUR. THE FAMED *TIGER PRINCE.*

I have traveled far from my palace to ask that you join me on a noble quest. It is time for you to be a hero.

I'LL DO ANYTHING YOU SAY.
NOW, ARTHUR, HOLD ON... JUST...

My lad, I will not mince words. Your friend Eamonn has done some terrible things.
WHAT?

It is true. He killed his brothers when he was young. And he has, in effect, killed Nellie Duncan as well.
... BUT SHE'S NOT DEAD *YET*, IS SHE?

It is only a matter of time, young adventurer. Eamonn is dangerous. He does not mean to be, but he must be controlled for the good of the world.

BUT WHAT CAN I DO, YOUR MAJESTY?
SHELLEY HAYES HAS THE ABILITY TO SEND HIM TO A SAFE PLACE WHERE HE CANNOT HARM ANYONE EVER AGAIN.

"WHERE?"
"WHY, MY KINGDOM, OF COURSE. YOU MUST HELP ME BRING HER HERE SO THAT I MAY CONVINCE HER TO SEND EAMONN TO ME."

JUST A MINUTE...
IS IT ALL TRUE, BUDDY?

... BUDDY?

EAMONN'LL BE ALL RIGHT, LI'L GUY.
He will be perfectly safe. We know he is not to blame. We just wish not to cause any more suffering.

Tomorrow night, think only about her. I will do the same. That will bring her here so that we may confer.

And once you awaken, you can speak of this to no one. Not even Ms. Hayes herself.
YES, YOUR MAJESTY! I UNDERSTAND!

REMEMBER, WHEN YOU GO TO BED TOMORROW... THINK ONLY OF HER.
I WILL! I PROMISE I WILL!

YOU WERE RIGHT. IT WAS A GOOD IDEA TO INVOLVE YOUR FRIEND. I FORGIVE YOU FOR LETTING THE "OTHER" ESCAPE.
WHAT DID YOU DO?! HOW DID YOU DO IT?!

HIS MIND IS YOUNG AND EASILY MOLDED. I JUST "BECAME" A MORE COMFORTING FELINE PRESENCE FOR HIM THAN I THOUGHT WOULD BE POSSIBLE.

THAT STILL DOESN'T EXPLAIN –
WE BOTH HAVE A UNIQUE FELINE CONNECTION. THAT IS ALL YOU NEED TO KNOW.

... FINE. IF YOU WERE GOING TO DO SOMETHING LIKE THAT, WE COULD'VE DISCUSSED THIS AHEAD OF TIME.
THIS SOLUTION CAME TO ME THERE AND THEN.

BUT THE WAY YOU DECEIVED HIM — I TOLD YOU I DIDN'T WANT HIM TO BE HURT.
DON'T BE SO MELODRAMATIC.

DO YOU WANT TO CONQUER THIS EAMONN CRISIS OR NOT?
BESIDES, I'VE DONE YOU A FAVOR.
I'VE DEFLECTED THIS ENTIRE SITUATION FROM YOU. YOU WERE JUST AS UNAWARE AS ARTHUR WAS.
THEREFORE YOU WON'T LOSE ARTHUR'S TRUST SHOULD ANYTHING GO WRONG.

TIRA PRN'T

EAMONN!

BIJOU SAID THAT BOTH OF YOU WERE ATTACKED BY RACCOONS THIS MORNING! ARE YOU ALL RIGHT?
YES. I WAS BITTEN, SO MARCEL'S COMING TO COLLECT ME SO THAT I CAN GET A RABIES SHOT.
WHAT HAPPENED?

OH, EVA... I DON'T WANT THERE TO BE A FUSS, BUT I THINK SOMETHING IS GOING WRONG HERE. THIS HAS HAPPENED BEFORE.

"WHEN I WAS A PUPPY, ONCE IN A WHILE THE ODD SQUIRREL OR HARE WOULD BECOME AGITATED WITH US SEEMINGLY FOR NO REASON. I THOUGHT NOTHING OF IT AT THE TIME."

BUT NOW IT'S CLEAR TO ME. WHAT WE'RE DOING CAN INDIRECTLY AFFECT THE MINDS OF WILD ANIMALS.
I WISH I'D WORKED THAT OUT BEFORE...

BUT AS YOU KNOW THAT'S JUST HOW OUR BRAVE NEW WORLD ROLLS.

IT'S UNBELIEVABLE. BUT IT'S TRUE. I KNOW IT IS. SO WHAT DO I DO?

I MEAN, FLUFFYPANTS IS RIGHT...

IF I TRIED TO BLACKMAIL THEM THE TRADITIONAL WAY, THERE'S NO REASON WE COULDN'T ALL BE SNUFFED IN A HOT MINUTE. ANIMALS' LIVES ARE CHEAP.

STILL... THIS DIRT IS TOO DAMN GOOD.

IF I NOW POSSESS QUENBY'S "PSYCHIC" ABILITIES, IT'D BE A CRIME TO LET 'EM GO TO WASTE.
ESPECIALLY SINCE, IF I PLAY MY CARDS RIGHT, THIS COULD KEEP THE BESTS AND THEIR LAWYERS OUT OF OUR FUR PERMANENTLY.

WELL... EVEN IF THE CHOSEN SOULS ARE IDIOTS, ONE OF 'EM MIGHT HAVE SOME INSIGHT. TIME TO SHAKE UP THE SERMON.

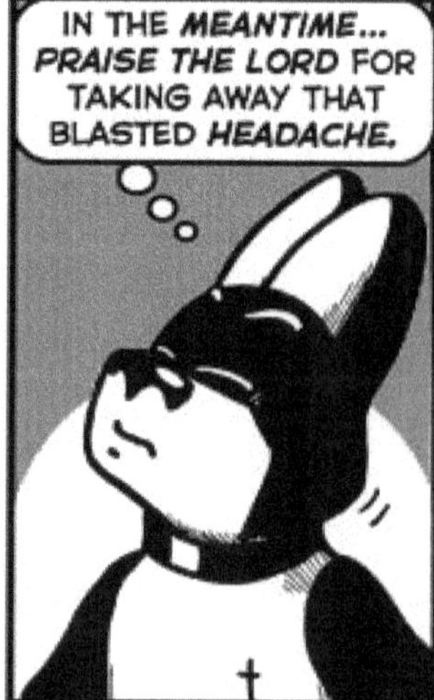

IN THE MEANTIME... PRAISE THE LORD FOR TAKING AWAY THAT BLASTED HEADACHE.

... NOPE. NOW THAT I'M HERE, I STILL HAVE NO IDEA HOW TO DO THIS WITHOUT AGITATING THE WILDLIFE.
EVA!

WHAT IS IT?
BUDDY'S EVIDENTLY HERE AGAIN.

I'M GETTING REALLY TIRED OF BUDDY THINKING I'M STILL JUST A PUPPY.
ER...

I DON'T THINK THIS IS BUDDY'S DOING.

HIYA! WHADDYA THINK?
DO YOU LIKE IT??

IT'S YOU! I FREED YOU! WHY ARE YOU STILL HERE?
DON'T YOU WANT ME AROUND?

WELL... BUT YOU'RE FREE NOW. DON'T YOU WANT TO GO BACK TO YOUR FRIENDS?
"FRIENDS?"

YOUR... UM... "KIND?"
"OH. THEY AREN'T FRIENDS. WE DON'T REALLY THINK IN THOSE TERMS."

... BUT I THOUGHT YOU WANTED TO BE FREE.
YOU REALLY DON'T REMEMBER ME, DO YOU?

...HA! I GUESS YOU WOULDN'T, SINCE I DIDN'T SHOW MYSELF. BUT I'VE BEEN THERE WITH YOU FROM THE BEGINNING. I HELPED MAKE ALL THOSE WORLDS THAT MADE YOUR HUMAN GUESTS HAPPY!

... WHAAAAAAAAAAAAAT ... ?

I LIKE YOU A LOT.
I'VE ALWAYS LIKED YOU!
AND SINCE YOU SAVED ME, I HOPE WE CAN BE "FRIENDS," AS YOU PUT IT!

"For thine is the kingdom and the power and the glory, forever and ever. Amen."

... CHOSEN SOULS. EVEN AS WE BEGIN OUR BLESSED JOURNEY TO THE ULTIMATE KINGDOM OF HEAVEN, THE WORLD OUTSIDE CHALLENGES US WITH MANY TRIALS.
BUT IT IS SAID IN THE BOOK OF ISAIAH, CHAPTER 40, VERSE 31, THAT EVEN THE WEAK, AS THEY HOPE IN THE KING OF HEAVEN, WILL RENEW THEIR STRENGTH.

IT IS IN THIS HOPE THAT I COME TO YOU. FOR...
... FOR I ...
... I'M SORRY, WHO IS THAT?

... OH! THIS IS MY OWNER! I CONVINCED HIM TO COME!

MOVE OUT OF THE WAY PLEASE.

... HOW?!
... I DON'T KNOW.

I'D ALWAYS HOPED HE'D SHOW UP, AND WITH A LOT OF EFFORT, I MADE IT HAPPEN!
WHAT IS THIS PLACE?

THE KINGDOM OF HEAVEN.
OH... REALLY? 'CAUSE IT DOESN'T SEEM ALL THAT... LIKE...

ARE YOU CALLING ME A LIAR?
"NO, NO..."

IF YOU SAY THIS IS THE KINGDOM OF HEAVEN, THEN THAT'S WHAT THIS IS.
LISTEN TO HIM, BUZZ. HE'S VERY SMART.

DO YOU KNOW WHO I AM?
THE REVEREND.

YOU'RE GOING TO LEAD US ALL TO THE ULTIMATE KINGDOM OF HEAVEN.

THAT... THAT'S RIGHT. AND I ASSUME... YOU'D BE WILLING TO DO ANYTHING TO MAKE THAT HAPPEN, WOULDN'T YOU?
OF COURSE! OF COURSE! I WANT TO JOIN YOU!

"... STAY HERE, THEN."
CLAMP!

EVERYBODY STAY RIGHT WHERE YOU ARE. I WISH TO TALK TO THIS CHOSEN SOUL FOR JUST A FEW MINUTES.

SO... ALL THOSE ENVIRONMENTS... WERE ESSENTIALLY CREATED BY THOSE ALIEN BEINGS. EVEN HIKARU'S "BRIDGE" WAS PROBABLY MADE BY THAT DRAGON WHO SENT US DOWN THE "BLACK HOLE."
YES... AND BOGS... HE EVEN SAID HE WOULDN'T "TAKE ME ANYWHERE" AGAIN.

WELL, EXCEPT TO WICKLOW, I SUPPOSE.
PROBABLY HIS IDEA OF A "GOING-AWAY" PRESENT.

WHAT AM I GONNA DO? I MEAN... HE SEEMS NICE 'N' ALL FOR SURE, BUT ALL THAT'S HAPPENED... I DUNNO...
"ALL THAT'S HAPPENED" IS THE VERY REASON WE NEED TO BUILD AN ALLIANCE.

WE'RE LEARNING AMAZING THINGS ABOUT THESE BEINGS. IF WE TRY TO WORK WITH THEM — CAREFULLY — WE COULD FIND OUT SO MUCH MORE ABOUT WHAT WE'RE COPING WITH.

"WHY DON'T WE SEE JUST WHAT THESE FOLKS HAVE TO OFFER?"

ARE YOU SERIOUS?!
I COULD HAVE SUGGESTED HE KILL HIMSELF FOR THE GLORY OF GOD AND HE WOULD HAVE DONE IT.

AND YOU'RE EXCITED ABOUT THIS?! GOOD LORD, WHAT IS GOING ON HERE?!
"WHAT'S GOING ON?!"

TWO DAYS AGO I DIDN'T EVEN KNOW WE COULD BRING HUMANS IN, AND NOW WE APPARENTLY CAN, AND WE'RE IN CONTROL. WE'RE. IN. CONTROL.
BUT IT'S SO... SO WRONG...

WHY DO YOU CARE?! HAVEN'T THEY BEEN STIFLING YOUR CAREER?!
WHAT HAVE THEY EVER DONE TO EARN ANY LOYALTY FROM YOU?!

... I'LL BELIEVE IT WHEN I SEE IT.
WATCH THE BANK ACCOUNT, KINGMAKER. YOU'LL BELIEVE IT THEN.

"ARE WE SURE SHELLEY HAYES WILL SEE THIS 'TIGER PRINCE'?"

"AS LONG AS YOU DO YOUR PART TO KEEP UP THE ILLUSION AND NOT PLAY GAMES, SHE'LL SEE WHAT ARTHUR SEES."

"ALL RIGHT. JUST DON'T HURT EITHER OF THEM."
"FOR THE LAST TIME..."

...NO ONE WILL GET HURT.

"Welcome, Ms. Hayes..."

... to the world of your dreams.

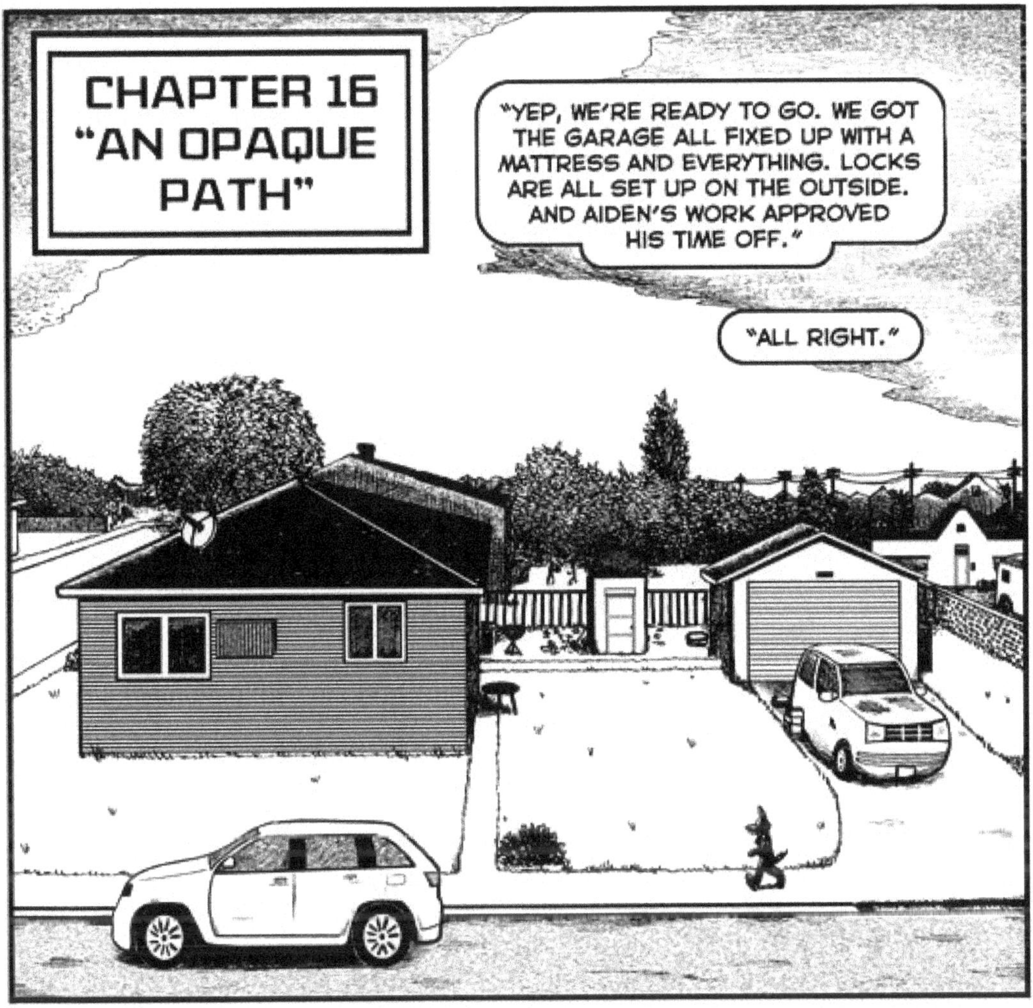

CHAPTER 16
"AN OPAQUE PATH"

YOU BLUFF TOO OFTEN, HE'LL CALL YOU ON IT. HE'S NOT AN IDIOT.
WE UNDERSTAND. MAYBE WE PLAY "GOOD COP, BAD COP."

... SURE.

JUST GET HIM TO YOUR PLACE AND MAKE SURE HE'S LOCKED UP BUT FED AND COMFORTABLE. WE'LL TAKE CARE OF THE REST.
OKAY...

IF YOU DON'T MIND US ASKIN', WHAT IS IT YOU'RE GOING TO DO?

... WE'RE GOING TO DESTROY THE DEEP-STATE-BASED SATAN THAT'S TAKEN HOLD OF HIM.

AW... THAT'S AWFUL NICE O' YA.
THANK YOU. COMING FROM TWO OF GOD'S BLESSED CHILDREN, THAT MEANS A LOT TO ME.

SO, UH... ANYWAY, WE LEAVE TOMORROW. THE HAYES WOMAN CALLED 'N' TOLD US THE DOG'D BE READY BY THEN.
GOOD. GODSPEED, ILLUMINATI CHASERS.
BEEP

IS THAT *REALLY* THE ANCIENT ALEXANDRIA LIBRARY?
JUST AS IT WAS A LONG TIME AGO!

IN AN EARLY PART OF WHAT EUROPEAN SCHOLARS CALL THE "COMMON ERA!"
I'M VERY IMPRESSED, MAGS.

OH, I FORGOT TO MENTION... HE WANTS TO CHANGE HIS NAME TO "KILROY."
DOMO ARIGATO, MISTER RISOTTO!

... YOU'RE VERY STRANGE.
DO YOU REALLY THINK WE'LL FIND ANYTHING OF VALUE IN HERE?

SURE! THIS'LL CONTAIN MOST OF WHAT YOU NEED TO KNOW! AND I CAN EVEN HELP TRANSLATE! AFTER ALL, I'M *KILROY! KILROY!*
UM... OKAY, THANK YOU, KILROY. LET'S HAVE A LOOK AROUND.

http://www.-paypal.com
zelle
VENMO
Your transfer has completed successfully
SO WHAT DO YOU SEE?
ANOTHER FIVE HUNDRED DOLLARS HAS COME IN SINCE YESTERDAY.

AND ...?
IS THIS TAXABLE?!

OF COURSE NOT, WE'RE A CHURCH.
THAT'S WHY I BROUGHT THIS TO YOUR ATTENTION. I NEED YOU TO GET ALL THE FORMS TAKEN CARE OF, THE IRS, ALL THAT...
"THIS WILL BRING US MORE ATTENTION THAN WE NEED."

AND IT STILL DOESN'T SOLVE THE PROBLEM OF BEST'S HEIRS WANTING US OUT OF HERE! YOUR MEETINGS WITH THE BEST FAMILY AND THEIR LAWYERS HAVEN'T DONE SQUAT!!

"SMACK" NOT YET. THE TIME ISN'T RIGHT FOR THAT.
WHAT?

DO YOU THINK I'M ACTUALLY NEGOTIATING ANYTHING DURING THESE RIDICULOUS MEETINGS?!
THE WHOLE POINT IS TO CONNECT WITH EVERY HUMAN INVOLVED, TO GET TO KNOW THEM, TO BE ABLE TO UNDERSTAND THEM FULLY 24/7.
THIS IS HOW WE GET THE MONEYGRUBBERS OUT OF THE TEMPLE AND IN TO THE KINGDOM OF HEAVEN.

KNOCK KNOCK
COME IN!

"COME ON, HORACE, IT'S TIME TO GO HOME."
"HELLO, MRS. YOUNG."
SHIFT
SHUFFLE
SHIFT

I'LL SEE YOU NEXT WEEK, HORACE.

...SCRABBLE THIS TIME?
YEAH, HE MOSTLY JUST SHUFFLED THE TILES AROUND.

ARE YOU SURE YOU WANT TO KEEP DOING THIS? I MEAN, MRS. YOUNG APPRECIATES IT, BUT IF HE HASN'T OPENED UP BY NOW...
HE WILL. I KNOW HE WILL. I'D REALLY LIKE TO STICK WITH THIS IF IT'S OKAY WITH YOU.

NO SKIN OFF MY NOSE! IT'S ONLY A HALF-HOUR OUT OF YOUR WEEK, AFTER ALL.
CLICK

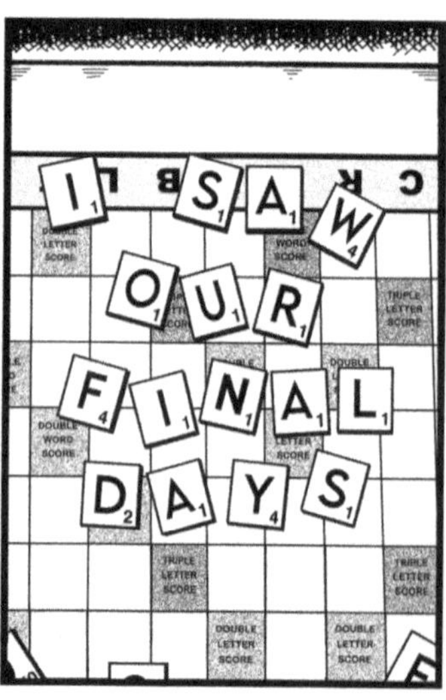
I SAW
OUR
FINAL
DAYS

"THE CLERIC CLASS OF KEMET - EGYPT HAVE ELEVATED BASE ANIMALS INTO GODS. BY DOING SO THESE DARK DENIZENS OF THE SOIL'S IGNOBLE ACTIONS HAVE FALLEN AWAY INTO THE EMPIRE OF MEMORY."
"THEY NOW WALK UPON TWO LEGS, ENGAGE IN VULGAR AND OFTEN GARBLED SPEECH, AND PRIOR TO THE GLORIOUS VICTORY OF CAESAR AT THE BATTLE OF ACTIUM, INHABITED THE TEMPLES AS HONORED GUESTS."
WE KNOW A LOT OF THIS.
AH, BUT PAY ATTENTION NOW.

"THEIR EXPULSION FROM PTOLEMY'S HOUSES OF WORSHIP WAS INDUCED BY THEIR INSISTENCE THAT THE GODS SPOKE UNTO THEM DIRECTLY DURING THEIR RESTING HOURS, THAT THEY ALONE HAD THE GUIDANCE OF JUPITER, OF JUNO, OF MINERVA, AND OF MARS."

"BELIEVING SUCH SPEECH TO INDUCE A PHLEGMATIC IMBALANCE, UNDER THE COMMAND OF THE PREFECT, THE PROCURATORS DROVE THEM OUT AND EXECUTED THOSE THAT CONTINUED TO SPEAK IN A MANNER SEDITIOUS TO OUR MOST GLORIOUS CAESAR."

THANK YOU FOR FINDING US SUCH A CONCISE SUMMARY.
ANYTHING TO HELP! AND AS YOU CAN SEE, WE'VE BEEN AROUND A LONG TIME.

YES, THAT APPEARS TO BE TRUE...
I DON'T WANT TO SOUND SCEPTICAL, BUT HOW DO WE KNOW ANY OF THAT'S ACCURATE?

I MEAN, EVEN WHEN BOGS WAS CREATING WORLDS, I HAD NO IDEA IF THOSE PLACES WERE "REAL" ...
OH, THEY HAVE TO BE!

WE DON'T HAVE ANY "IMAGINATION" TO "CREATE" SOMETHING NONEXISTENT!
WE DON'T EVEN WANT THAT!
EVERYTHING WE MANIFEST EITHER EXISTS NOW, EXISTED IN THE PAST, OR EXISTS AS A CONCEPT A LIFE FORM LIKE YOU CREATED!

... AND THAT THIRD ONE IS TRICKY, TOO.
I HOPE KAYLA WAS HAPPY WITH MY VERSION OF HER INSTRUMENT-LAND-THING ...
CHUCKLE SHE WAS.
WELL, I HAVE TO SAY THAT'S TRULY REMARKABLE, KILROY ...
I JUST WISH I KNEW HOW IT IS YOU CAN DO THIS.

"OH, I KNOW SOMEONE WHO COULD PROBABLY TELL YOU!"

YOU DO?!
THREE SOMEONES, IN FACT!

YOU MEAN, THREE OF YOUR SPECIES?
"OF COURSE."

YOU MIGHT CALL THEM SCHOLARS. WE HAVE NO USE FOR THEM.
WELL, WE CERTAINLY MIGHT!

DO THEY KNOW A LOT ABOUT THIS?
IT'S POSSIBLE. THOUGH I'M NOT SURE HOW MUCH YOU'LL GET OUT OF THEM. THEY HAVE NO USE FOR YOU.

... REALLY.
"YOU ARE PLAYTHINGS. THEY CONSIDER YOU FRIVOLOUS AND TRIVIAL."

MAYBE WE CAN CHANGE THEIR MINDS.
WELL, I SHALL ASK THEM IF THEY WILL MEET YOU! I'LL DO ANYTHING FOR MY FRIEND!
RUSTLE RUSTLE
?

SO... YOU'RE SERIOUS?

NO MORE OF THIS STALLING? YOU'LL GET OUT?
I'LL DO MORE THAN THAT. I THINK YOU'LL BE VERY SATISFIED BY TOMORROW.

OH, THANK GOD. THIS WAS DRAGGING ON WAY TOO LONG.
HOLD IT, "PREACHER PUP." WHAT DID YOU MEAN BY THAT?

I MEAN, YOU'LL GET WHAT YOU WANT. IF YOU'RE NOT HAPPY BY TOMORROW... YOU CAN CALL IN ALL YOUR LEGAL TROOPS TO EVICT ME.

DON'T THREATEN US WITH A GOOD TIME.
WHEN YOU NEXT SEE ME, I WILL NO LONGER BE OCCUPYING MR. BEST'S MANSION.

"... PREACHER PUP."
OH LORD, THIS WILL BE WORTH QUITTING SMOKING FOR.

DO WE HAVE TO DO THIS AGAIN? TITUS SAID HIS "ILLUMI-NUTTY CHASERS WERE ON THEIR WAY. ISN'T HAYES SUFFICIENTLY ON BOARD?
WE'VE LOST ANY CONTROL OF THE DOGS EAMONN'S ALREADY LOOSED UPON THIS PLANE. WE NEED TO ENSURE THAT TROUBLEMAKER IS LOCKED AWAY BEFORE HE BRINGS IN MORE.

I JUST WANT THIS TO END. PRUDENCE LA SALLE IS STILL BEING DIFFICULT.
SHE'S DOING WHAT SHE'S SUPPOSED TO, ISN'T SHE?

TITUS, DON'T ...
QUIET! THEY'RE ARRIVING.

Greetings!
FUCK YOU.

MS. HAYES! THAT'S THE TIGER PRINCE!
SHUT UP, CAT!!

IT IS NOT!! THE TIGER PRINCE IS FICTIONAL! THIS IS SOME GOD-FORSAKEN DEMON OUT TO DESTROY MY LIFE!!

I assure you, madam, there is no cause for—
SHUT UP!! I SAID I'D DO IT! THEY'RE COMING TOMORROW!!

ONCE I DO THIS, YOU HAVE TO LEAVE ME ALONE!! I'M BEHIND ON ALL MY DEADLINES BECAUSE I CAN'T FOCUS!!
MY EDITOR ACTUALLY CALLED ME TO ASK IF I WAS OKAY! BECAUSE I HAVE NEVER ONCE IN MY LIFE MISSED A DEADLINE!!

SHE CALLED ME! AND I HAD TO LIE!!
THIS WILL BE OUR LAST VISIT, MS. HAYES.

OUR... LAST... VISIT.
...I'M GOING TO SELL THE DAMN DOG. I TOLD YOU I WOULD. PLEASE. PLEASE. LEAVE ME ALONE.
...PLEASE.

TAKE IT EASY, BUDDY.
YES, WE'RE ONLY ONE STEP AWAY FROM GAINING CONTROL OF THIS CRISIS. AFTER ALL...

STOP!

YOU SAY "THIS IS WAR" ONE MORE TIME, YOU'RE HANDLING EAMONN ON YOUR OWN.

ALL RIGHT, ALL RIGHT... LET'S TAKE A BREATH HERE, FOLKS. THIS'LL ALL SOON BE OVER.

Chosen Souls!

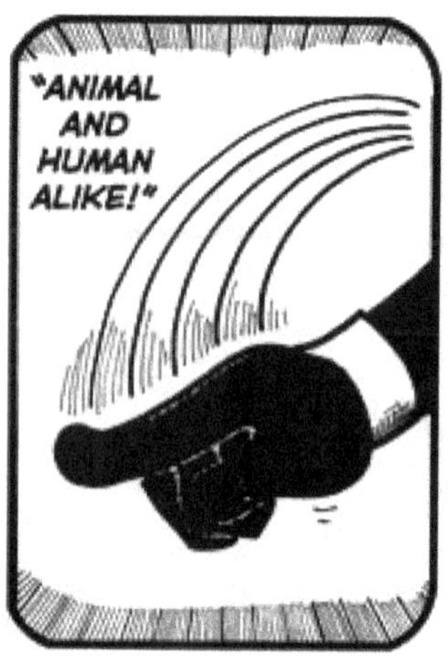

"ANIMAL AND HUMAN ALIKE!"

"YOUR DEVOTION TO THE LORD HAS BEEN IMMENSE, AND BECAUSE OF THIS, YOU SHALL KNOW THE GLORY OF SALVATION!"
HALLELUJAH!

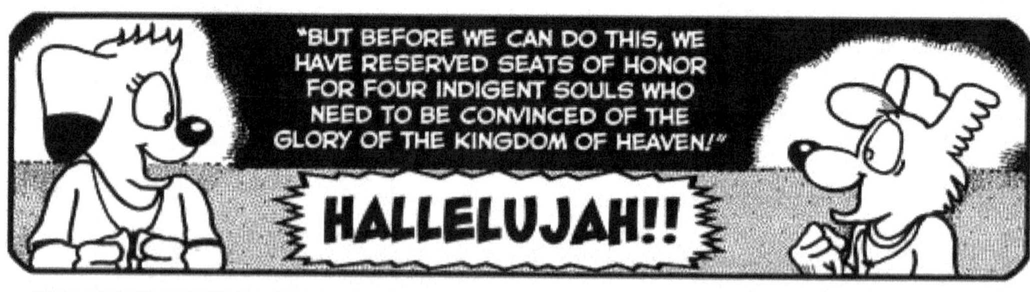

"BUT BEFORE WE CAN DO THIS, WE HAVE RESERVED SEATS OF HONOR FOR FOUR INDIGENT SOULS WHO NEED TO BE CONVINCED OF THE GLORY OF THE KINGDOM OF HEAVEN!"
HALLELUJAH!!

THEY NEED TO BE BROUGHT TO US TO BE CONVINCED THAT OUR HOLY JOURNEY MUST CONTINUE! THAT NOTHING SHALL HINDER US IN OUR QUEST FOR THE ULTIMATE KINGDOM OF HEAVEN!
HALLELUJAH!!
SO KINDLY WAIT, GENTLE SOLDIERS, WHILE I INVITE THEM INTO HEAVEN ...
... SO THAT THEY MAY HEAR THE WORDS OF GOD AND BE HEALED!
HALLELUJAH!!

WHAT
IN --
WHAT'S
GOING ON?!
LOOK!
"HELLO,
WASTELAND
WANDERERS."

MY FIRST ORDER
OF BUSINESS
IS TO INFORM
YOU THAT THE
HOUSE YOU ONCE
KNEW AS THE
GIDEON BEST
MANSION ...

... WILL HENCEFORTH
BE KNOWN AS THE
TEMPLE OF THE
CHOSEN SOULS.

ISN'T THAT
WONDERFUL?
BLESS YOU ALL FOR
MAKING THIS SACRIFICE!!
YOU'RE
GOING TO LOVE
THE REVEREND!
JUST LIKE WE
DO!

WE KNOW YOU'RE GOING TO WARN HIM. WE WANT TO SEE HIM *DIE.*

HELP!

DON'T SAY A WORD OR WE'LL KILL YOU.
WHAT THE HELL IS GOING ON HERE?!

THAT ONE ... THAT MONSTER ... IS GOING TO DIE ... AND THERE'S NOTHING YOU CAN DO ABOUT IT.
WHAT?

BIJOU! SOMEONE'S COMING TO GET EAMONN! THEY SAID HE WOULDN'T GET HURT BUT I DON'T BELIEVE THEM!
I TOLD YOU TO SHUT UP!!

... BECAUSE THEY'RE HURTING MS. HAYES!!

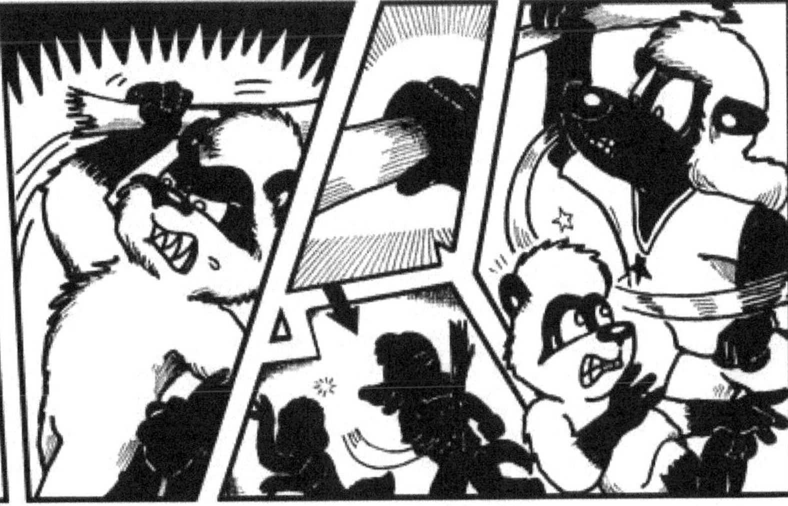

GET OUT!! ALL OF YOU!!
GET OUT!!!

IT DOESN'T MATTER WHAT YOU DO ANYMORE!! HE WILL DIE!!!

WHAT... IS... GOING... ON.
ARE YOU ALL RIGHT?
OH, BIJOU...

I WASN'T SUPPOSED TO TELL YOU, BUT...
BUDDY CAME TO ME IN THAT "DREAM WORLD" YOU GUYS ALL MET IN, AND HE SOMEHOW MADE THE "TIGER PRINCE" FROM MS. HAYES' STORIES APPEAR ...

THEY TOLD ME EAMONN HAD DONE SOME AWFUL STUFF AND THAT THEY WERE GONNA TAKE HIM TO THE TIGER PRINCE'S KINGDOM!

SO THEY TOLD MS. HAYES SHE HAD TO SELL HIM TO SOMEBODY! THEY SAID EAMONN WOULDN'T BE HURT, BUT AFTER SEEING WHAT THEY'VE DONE TO MS. HAYES...

"... I DON'T BELIEVE THEM ANYMORE!!"

YOU'RE RIGHT NOT TO TRUST BUDDY ANYMORE. I'M SO SORRY I DIDN'T TELL YOU.
SO WHAT DOES THIS MEAN?

I MEAN, I ALREADY CAN FEEL IT! EAMONN'S IN DANGER!
GIVE ME A SECOND... I CAN'T THINK...
HOLD IT!!!

... THANK YOU. MAY I?

NOW, LAD... FIRST, ARE YOU SURE YOU'RE ALL RIGHT?
I'M FINE! BUT YOU NEED TO ESCAPE!

I DON'T KNOW WHO YOU'RE GOING TO BE SOLD TO, BUT SEEING HOW THEY WENT AND HURT MS. HAYES, IT CAN'T BE ANYONE GOOD! YOU SHOULD RUN AWAY!

ARE THEY THE REASON THE RACCOONS SAID HE WAS GOING TO DIE?
I DON'T KNOW! I DON'T WANNA IMAGINE BUDDY KILLING ANYBODY!

I'M NOT KIDDING HERE, EAMONN. YOU'RE IN DANGER. I FEEL IT.
WELL, PECULIARLY ENOUGH...

... I DON'T.

I'D LIKE TO SEE WHAT'S GOING TO HAPPEN.

ARE YOU CRAZY? WE DON'T KNOW WHO THESE "BUYERS" ARE OR WHAT THIS "TIGER PRINCE"-BUDDY BROMANCE HAS IN MIND FOR YOU!
WELL, YOU KNOW...

... I'D ACTUALLY BE DELIGHTED TO FIND OUT.

LATER THAT MORNING ...
... THERE SHE IS.

ARE YOU THE ONES COMING ... COMING FOR THE IRISH SETTER?
YUP.

OKAY, I THINK WE HAVE IT ALL HERE --
I DON'T WANT YOUR MONEY. HE'S IN THERE. GO GET HIM.
NOT YET!

MOVE ASIDE, ALL RIGHT?
SHELLEY... I'M SO SORRY ABOUT WHAT THEY DID TO YOU. IT WAS WRONG.

I DON'T KNOW WHAT YOU'RE TALKING ABOUT. MOVE ASIDE AND LET THEM THROUGH.
PLEASE... I JUST WANT TO ASK A COUPLE OF QUESTIONS.

MOVE ASIDE AND LET THEM HAVE THE DOG, OR I'LL THROW YOU ALL OUT!!
...INCLUDING THAT CAT!!
"EVA ..."

... SHELLEY'S BEEN THROUGH ENOUGH. I'M COMING ALONG QUIETLY.

YOU PROMISED ME I COULD FIND OUT WHO THESE PEOPLE ARE!
I DON'T THINK IT MAKES ANY DIFFERENCE.

IT'S BUDDY AND THAT SOCIETY BIJOU'S ON ABOUT THAT WANTS ME.
YOU WON'T HURT HIM, RIGHT?

WHAT?! OF COURSE NOT!
WE'RE SUPPOSED TO TREAT HIM LIKE ROYALTY!
Toby Keith's

... I'LL JUST GET MY NIGHTSHIRT ...

... EAMONN.

I WANT YOU TO LISTEN TO ME. NOW.

IT DOESN'T MATTER WHAT YOU FEEL...
YOU ARE IN DANGER.
AND YOU SHOULD NOT DO THIS.

WHILE I'M NOT AFTER UNDERMINING ANYTHING YOU'RE FEELING ...
QUENBY ...

I THINK YOU'RE NOT SEEING HOW THIS MIGHT BE VALUABLE FOR ALL OF US. IN FACT, I PREFER TO CONSIDER THIS A TEST.

WHAT KIND OF TEST?
THAT I DON'T KNOW.

... APART FROM IT BEING ONE I CAN PASS.

" ... MAYBE WE SHOULD INTRODUCE OURSELVES? MY NAME'S EAMONN."
"OOH, DON'T YOU HAVE THE CUTEST ACCENT! YOU'RE LIKE A LITTLE ORANGE LEPRECAUN!"
"AHEM ... YEAH. THAT'S HAZEL. I'M AIDEN.
AND DON'T WORRY, DOG ... WE'LL TREAT YA REAL GOOD."

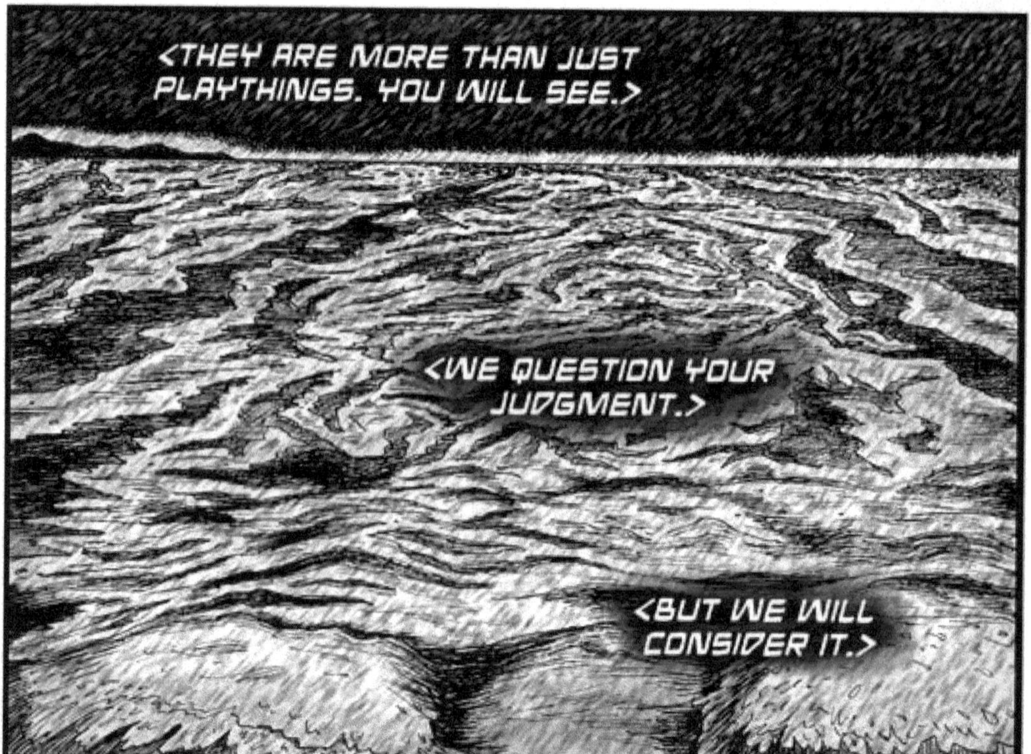

<THEY ARE MORE THAN JUST PLAYTHINGS. YOU WILL SEE.>
<WE QUESTION YOUR JUDGMENT.>
<BUT WE WILL CONSIDER IT.>

TO BE
CONTINUED...

www.furplanet.com